# BIRDS TALK

*A guide to some common British birds
in which the birds tell their own story*

Edward Cowie
www.edward-cowie.com

Birds Talk Press
Devon

BIRDS TALK
Copyright © Edward Cowie 2001

ISBN 0 9544690 0 3

Published 2003 by
BIRDS TALK PRESS LTD
Beckstones
Buckfast Road, Buckfastleigh
Devon TQ11 0EA

Printed in Great Britain by York Publishing
Services for Birds Talk Press

# BIRDS TALK

*A guide to some common British birds in which the birds tell their own story*

*To  Heather*
*The best of natural wonders*
*and to my two daughters,*
*Anita and Virginia*

*Acknowledgements*

Many thanks to Heather for hours of patient listening and editing. To my daughters, Anita and Virginia, thanks for listening and laughing in all the right places. To Corrie Jeffery, without whose vigorous support and encouragement this book would have never found its way to print. And to the following, who will know how they impacted on this book, my heartfelt thanks: John and Barbara Wilson, Sue Kay, Judy Lowe and Brian Goodwin. Thanks also to Bill, for the Foreword.

Finally to the RSPB for providing me with endless resources for sensual pleasure with wild birds.

## Foreword by Bill Oddie

There is a very old song I remember on the radio when I was a kid. 'I talk to the trees, but they don't hear what I say', was the first line. I seem to recall that we unsentimental schoolboys were in the habit of changing that to 'I talk to the trees, that's why they put me away!' But, as it happens, I have a confession to make: I do talk to the trees! In fact - and you can call me a nutter if you like - when I am out in the countryside, I do not only talk to the trees, I also talk to flowers, insects, animals and of course birds, which are what I'm mainly looking for and at. Birdwatching has been my hobby since childhood and it is now my job (well, making TV programmes about birds is anyway).

So, yes, I'll admit it, I often talk to wildlife. Although I have never ever had a reply. Not once has a bird ever talked back to me. On the other hand, I reckon I have heard them talking to each other. After all, what are bird songs and bird calls if not a language? We even understand some of it. We recognise when a male is singing to impress a female. Or when a bird gives an 'alarm call' when there is a predator approaching; or a 'contact call' when a flock is flying high on migration.

But do birds actually have conversations or opinions about themselves, the world, or indeed us humans? Well, all I can say is I'd like to think so. I would also like to think that birds could write and publish a book. And if they could... maybe this is it.

(Even if they did need a little help from Professor Cowie. Any chance of a quick course in 'Birdish', Prof?)

Bill Oddie

## About the Author

Edward Cowie has an international reputation as both composer and painter. His music has been played and recorded all over the world and as an exhibiting painter, his watercolours and oils are in public and private collections in more than twenty countries. He has also worked as a conductor with many major orchestras and ensembles throughout the world.

He has made several television films including his acclaimed BBC2 film on Leonardo da Vinci. He wrote and recorded two major radio series for ABCFM, Australia, one of which being *Voices of the Land*, a natural history of sound.

Edward Cowie has been appointed as the First Artist in Residence with the Royal Society for the Protection of Birds 2002-5, and also the First Composer in Association with the BBC Singers in London, 2002-5.

All of Cowie's music and visual art is directly inspired by the living world in general, birds in particular, and he remains a committed and obsessive observer of nature. He has held professorships in the UK, Australia, Germany and the USA and is currently Professor and Director of Research at Dartington College of Arts in Devon, England.

He lives with his Australian painter wife in a house by the side of the River Dart in south Devon, where he continues to compose, paint and write more books on the living world.

How do-hoo yoo-hoo doo! It gives me great pleasure too-hoo welcome yoo-hoo all too-hoo this boo-hook in which we birds tell yoo-hoo all about ourselves in our own way. Of course we couldn't have done this all on our own. We had too-hoo have a little help from one of yoo-hoo hoomans. In order too-hoo doo-hoo this, I made sure that I found a hooman whoo-hoo really cared about us birds and whoo-hoo was prepared too-hoo be very quiet and just listen. Some of yoo-hoo hoomans are not very good at being quiet, but the one I chose certainly is.

It was all so easy really. Yoo-hoo see, I live in Devon, quite close too-hoo the River Dart. During the daylight hours, my wife and I sleep in the top of a great big larch tree. We have lovely views across a big valley with the river running throo-hoo it. It just so happens that there is a big quarry right behind our residence. The top of that quarry is just about the same height as the perch where we sleep. There is a little pathway that winds its way throo-hoo thickets of blackthorns and brambles, and from where we sit, we sometimes get goo-hood views of hoomans going for walks up that little path.

There's one hooman that we have seen more of than any other. He takes his two-hoo dogs for a walk some-times on that path, and last year he and his wife were often picking blackberries, so we got too-hoo know him quite well really. Yoo-hoo know, we birds have ways of knowing whether or not a hooman is one that we can trust. This one, we felt we coo-hood definitely trust. Once I saw that he came just too-hoo draw and paint nature and I realised that he was loo-hooking at me throo-hoo those funny black things just because he was curious. I felt that I coo-hood let him in on a great secret.

So I did.

One evening last spring, my wife and I were just about too-hoo wake up. Yoo-hoo know, just stretching the odd feather or two-hoo and opening and closing our beaks in great big yawns - we like doing that! Well, I reckon we have great hearing, but too-hoo be honest, we simply didn't notice that he was sitting only a few flaps away from us. Yes, just sitting there and loo-hooking right at us.

Not that he was a stranger too-hoo us, but he seemed even more interested in us than usual, so I decided too-hoo take a little flight over his head too-hoo have a peek at what he was up too-hoo. Imagine my surprise when I saw that he was actually making a drawing of the pair of us in our residence? It wasn't a bad drawing either. And what was even more interesting was the fact that he was also doo-hooing some very strange drawings of things that loo-hooked like a lot of little dots, squiggles and lines. When I saw that, I just had too-hoo hoot, so I did. And doo-hoo yoo-hoo know what he did then? He started to draw the noise I just made, and then he put those funny things on the ends of his wings too-hoogether (I think yoo-hoo call them hands) and started too-hoo hoot, just like me! Yoo-hoo coo-hood have knocked me out of the sky with a feather!

That night, my wife and I hunted as yoo-hoosual, but when we got back too-hoo the residence in the great larch, we sat and hooted about this strange hooman. I'm a tawny owl yoo-hoo see, and I'm far from stoo-hoopid. I worked it all out by myself. This hooman was actually trying too-hoo write down what we birds sing. He was trying too-hoo understand what my wife and I were saying too-hoo each other. Well, my wife and I hooted and hooted too-hoogether and we came too-hoo a decision that was hard too-hoo come too-hoo, but we now know was a goo-hood one. We decided that if this hooman really wanted too-hoo know what we were hooting about, we woo-hood show him our special secret.

So we did.

Now I am sure that yoo-hoo hoomans know what an oak tree is. Well, doo-hoo yoo-hoo? Goo-hood, I'm glad about that. Well, what yoo-hoo don't perhaps know is that oak trees are very special trees. The really old ones are the most special of all. Most old oak trees have got great big holes in them. Why, some birds even nest in them, my relatives included. Here's the big secret. If yoo-hoo got inside one of these really old oaks, and if a bird came and sang into-hoo that hole yoo-hoo would be able too-hoo hear for the first time *exactly* what we are saying! Yes, really - troo-hoo!

Yoo-hoo see, oak trees are magic trees, and they have something in them that we birds call a *Birdogram*. Don't ask me how it works 'cos that's a secret that we didn't even share with Edward Cowie, whoo-hoo is the hooman that we chose too-hoo make this boo-hook possible. We know that yoo-hoo hoomans are clever too-hoo, and that yoo-hoo have special machines that can record sounds. How clever of yoo-hoo by the way! So exactly how did we make contact with Edward? That's a nice story too-hoo.

Not long after my wife and I decided that we woo-hood choo-hoose Edward too-hoo make a boo-hook for us, we sent messages too-hoo all the birds that we coo-hood think of whoo-hoo woo-hood be interested too-hoo chat with yoo-hoo all. We chose carefully. We wanted too-hoo make sure that these birds woo-hood be ones that yoo-hoo coo-hood see easily. Not that I like the word much, but I believe that yoo-hoo hoomans call such birds *common birds*. Common? Really! Well, I ask yoo-hoo - what a cheek!

Believe it or not, every bird we talked too-hoo (in Birdish of course), was more than keen too-hoo talk about their life too-hoo Edward, though one or two-hoo were a bit on the reluctant side. Shy, yoo-hoo see. We also realised that some of the birds were not going too-hoo be able too-hoo fly up too-hoo the big oak near us, so we found a way around that. Our big oak is very, very old yoo-hoo see, and last year, one of its branches fell off during a great big storm. It's not a big branch, but it is hollow. Because this branch comes from a Birdogram tree, it works just like one of yoo-hoo hooman's recorder thingies.

One morning, a few weeks later, Edward the hooman came too-hoo his little perch close too-hoo us. We knew he woo-hood come because he had been visiting the badgers the night before and the badgers have their home right in the roo-hoots of the old oak close by. In fact, Edward the hooman sat right next too-hoo this tree sometimes, and on this cold and frosty morning, there he was!

I knew that he woo-hood be very surprised to see me flying in the sunlight, especially right too-hoowards him, but I did just that. Yoo-hoo should have seen his face! I flew right over his head and perched on a dead branch in the magic oak tree. Somehow, I had too-hoo get him too-hoo put his head inside the tree, or I woo-hood never be able too-hoo talk too-hoo him. Oh, it was easy! All I did was fly inside the tree throo-hoo the big hole at the top and loo-hook down inside in the darkness too-hoo the bottom, where there was another big hole.

Well, yoo-hoo hoomans are a curious lot and I already knew how curious Edward the hooman was, so I just sat and waited. I don't think I'd blinked more than four times before he popped his head inside and loo-hooked up too-hoo where I was perched. The first thing he did was too-hoo make one of those strange sounds that yoo-hoo hoomans make when yoo-hoo get excited. He said, 'Wow!'

I can't remember the sound he made when I hooted my first Birdish words to him, but I doo-hoo remember that he shot his head out of the hole and back in again very fast. It seems that he was very shocked too-hoo find that I coo-hood actually speak too-hoo him and that he coo-hood too-hoo me as well. He kept on talking about some funny hooman called Doctor Doo-hoolittle or something like that. Too-hoo be honest at the time I had no idea what he was talking about, but I think I doo-hoo now.

We had a wonderful chat too-hoogether, and Edward agreed too-hoo yoo-hoose his special recorder thingy so that he coo-hood record us birds for his boo-hook. I told him too-hoo yoo-hoose the dead branch at the foo-hoot of the tree, and too-hoo take it everywhere with him when he was too-hoo meet each new bird. The bird talks intoo-hoo the Birdogram and Edward the hooman simply has too-hoo yoo-hoose his recorder thingy. He has done a great job, I must say. He told me only yesterday that he has read the boo-hook and that he only wished he coo-hood have had one like it when he was a little chick (whoops, sorry - hooman child).

So dear ones, on behalf of all of us and Edward includ-ed, we doo-hoo hope that yoo-hoo get as much fun from reading this boo-hook as we all did in making it. I'll be back later too-hoo talk too-hoo yoo-hoo all.

*Toohooooooooo* for now!

## Letter from Edward the Hooman

Dear All,

Well here it is, the book in which British birds talk about themselves in their own way. What an adventure it's been. I can well remember that first time when I heard Birdish spoken in the old oak tree above my house in Devon. As the excellent Bird Ambassador himself has often said (hooted without a Birdogram), 'you could have knocked me over with a feather!'

The Ambassador and I hooted and chatted about how to write this book down, and I must confess it wasn't always easy. Most birds don't talk quite the same way as we do, and I had to do a lot of checking with each bird to make sure that I'd got the spelling right. I'm sure you'll be able to cope with some of the odd words you'll find in here.

Lots of things really fascinated me about the birds I met, but most of all, I was surprised at how much character each had. I had no idea that birds spoke with accents just like us. When you read this, we don't mind if you can't read with the same accents that birds would speak in, but if you feel like having a go at Liverpudlian, Cockney and things like that, feel free! I've always tried to translate the Birdish into English just the way it came out on my recorder from the Birdogram. You'll just have to trust me, now won't you!

I expect you'll be wondering where you can get hold of a Birdogram yourselves. Now that is a tricky one. I'd have liked to have kept the one the Ambassador gave me, but I'm afraid it was only 'on loan'! Maybe, if like me you get very close to birds and show them how much you love them, you'll find a bird like the Ambassador who might lend you one. But let's face it, isn't it wonderful that one of them did lend it to me?

Just how can you get that close to birds?

Well, remember a few of these important things, it will help a lot:

Never go too close to a bird if it shows that it doesn't want you to approach.

Never go near a nest with a bird on it.

Never take eggs from a bird (it's against the law anyway!)

Always keep as quiet as you can when watching birds.

Don't move too quickly, it scares them.

Try to find out as much as you can about them by reading books like this and by going out into the fields and woods to watch them in their own living places.

If you can't get close enough for a good view, maybe think about saving up for a pair of binoculars.

Try to watch as many programmes as you can on TV, there are often some very good ones to see, and most birds have approved of what has been filmed.

Don't just look - *listen*!  There are great programmes on the radio too.

Keep a little diary about all your times with birds and if you can, even try to do a drawing of them, it helps you to remember them better.

Don't leave the kinds of food about that would make birds sick.

If you happen to like fishing, *never* leave any line about; it can entangle birds and kill them.

Always treat birds as you would your friends and loved ones, they'll love you right back.

It's okay to take pictures of them, but be patient and don't invade their privacy especially at nesting time.

Feed the garden birds in the winter from bird feeders and bird tables; you can offer them nuts, seeds, grained bread and fat, and don't be shy about feeding them all year round, it's quite safe.

If you need help getting to know more about birds, find someone who is an expert and ask them for some help.

At the end of this book, I have taken the liberty is listing an organisation that really cares a lot about birds. By joining it, you'll really be helping birds a lot and have heaps of fun at the same time. By the time you have read this book, you'll be quite an expert on a good number of British birds. Who knows, one of these days, I might get another loan of Ambassador owl's Birdogram, and we'll try to add some more to the list. Okay?

Have fun and lots of birdy good wishes to you all,

Edward

# Contents

## Part One
### Water Birds

## Part Two
### Garden Birds

*Part Three*
Woodland Birds

*Part Four*
Field Birds

*Part One*
Water Birds

Herbie the Grey Heron

## Herbie the Grey Heron

Hi there! I mean, hi *down* there. If you suffer from heights you'd better close your eyes and get someone else to read this, because I'm cruising at about two hundred feet at the moment. Now it seems to me that you might be wondering, 'hey... what's that big grey bird doing up there?' Well, I mean to say - what a silly question! Doing up here? Flying of course! Mind you, if you've got sharp eyes, you might have noticed that we sometimes hang about up here without flapping at all. Clever that. We have such big wings that we can glide you see. No, don't be silly, *you* can't glide - you haven't got wings.

Mind you, the next time we get one of those great big winds battering and bashing about, you know, the ones that break trees and take your toys for a whiz round the garden, open the buttons of your coat and face into the wind. Nice feeling, eh? I mean, you can lean right forward and still not fall over! See? the air is a bit thick as a matter of fact, thick enough to stop you from falling over when it moves that hard against you. Well, we herons can use that thick air to float through. It's that easy really - we either get up enough speed to rest our wings out straight and just glide, or sometimes we hit the heron-pot and get a thermal.

Oh ho, that got you wondering, didn't it? 'What's a thermal?' I hear you say. Well, you know about what happens to hot air? It rises, and the cold air comes down to take its place. This is easy, come on, think about it. The hot air is more excited than cold air. All the little atoms (you can't see them) dash about like crazy and make such a fuss that they take up more space between them than usual, so they make the air lighter. Well, that's about it really. The sun makes the air warm, it rises in great big blobs of warmth, and we herons take a ride on the uplift. It's a great feeeeeling!

Oh, I see, you want to know why we stay up here? Well, that's easy - we get hungry! It's all right for you lot, you can just get on your bikes (I don't mind bikes) or in your cars (I don't like cars), and whizz off down to those funny buildings full of yummy smells and buy your food in round things with labels on them. My Gaia, you don't even have to fish for fish, they come in funny plastic packs (we birds *hate* plastic packs!).

You just drop a lot of silly bits of paper or little round discs into peoples' hands and they actually *give* you the stuff to take home and eat. Well, lucky you! It ain't that easy for us birds. We don't have bikes, we don't have cars, and we don't have bank accounts!

So far as I'm concerned, I have to fly for my food. Come on, get wise! I like fish you see. Well, fish don't hang around in the same piece of water all the time you know. I mean, they'd get awfully bored, wobbling a few fins and just holding still in the same bit of river, their mouths hanging open in a yawning kind of way.

I mean, *they* have to eat as well, you know. I mean, they haven't got bikes or cars either, and they haven't got bank... whoops - getting a bit like a stuck CD here. Well, you know what I mean. Okay, get the picture? Fish move, *we* move. We eat all the fish in one spot and have to get to another spot to find some more. Hey, I don't want you to get the wrong idea, I don't just eat fish - boring just eating fish. I like anything that's small enough to get down my long throat.

Now there's a funny thing. Why do we herons have such long necks? It's okay, this is not a riddle. You hoomans are so good at riddles. We have long necks to look over things with. Same as you hoomans. What do you do to see further and better? Stand on your tippy-toes, eh? Well, that's why we have long necks - observation towers, if you know what I mean. It also helps to have a long neck for putting my beak into deeper water. And here's another funny thing - well I think it's funny - we also have long legs! I realise you probably haven't got all that close to one of us herons, so I'll help you a bit here. Have a look at your mum or dad's arms. If you put one hand on their finger tips, and the other hand where their elbow is, you'll get the picture. My legs are about that long. Honestly! Why? S'easy! Where do fish live? In rivers and streams and in the sea, of course, and is all water shallow? No way! See, it's like this - we like to fish in pretty shallow water, 'cos it's easy to see them there. But we also like to be able to wade in pretty deep because, well, because that's where some of the biggest fish live. So the longer the legs, the deeper we can get without making a lot of silly glugging noises and getting in too deep, if you know what I mean.

I mean, I'd look pretty stupid walking under water and trying to catch fish, wouldn't I? Leave that kind of fancy stuff to Deborah Dipper, or Gerald Goosesander. Well, I mean, I'm not a submarine.

Hey, want to look at my feet? Big, eh? Three toes pointing forward and one backwards. I don't know whether you've got one of those funny sticks with a light bulb on top in your house, but in case you are wondering why I have such big toes, well your lamp stick would fall over without toes now, wouldn't it?

And another thing, one of the best places for fish and crabs and frogs and lots of yummy water things is where there's a lot of that sticky gluggy brown stuff. I believe you call it mud? Have you ever tried to walk in mud? Hard eh? Ever got so stuck that you nearly lost a shoe? Bet you have! Well, that's not for Herbie boy. I've got such big feet that they spread out my weight and stop me from sinking. Neat!

By the way, how tall *am* I? Well, let's put it this way, if you were silly enough to leave a bit of fish on your plate at the dinner table, I'd snaffle that without you even noticing it, and you could put a serviette round my neck, and see it there just to prove what good manners I have! Not that I'd ever let you do it, but you'd have a hard job stretching your arms as wide as I can stretch my two wings. Why are my wings so big? Oh come on, surely you can work that one out for yourself.

Right, I've told you a bit about myself. Want to know a little more? Well, can you keep a secret? You can? Edward the hooman has gone for a little walk so I'll tell you something naughty. Are you sure you can keep a secret? Okay, I believe you.

I don't know if Edward the hooman has told you, but it's like this, see. He lives in Devon, where I do, right? Got a nice little place by the River Dart. Wow, what a place to eat. That river is greeeeeaaaaatttt! (Imagine me growling that in a low gruff kind of way, and you'll have some idea what my voice sounds like. Okay?)

Well, this Edward guy has a nice garden. His wife and he are often in there when I'm downriver, perched on a rock, looking for... well you know what! It's like this, see. Sometimes at night I fly a nice slow steady beat up the far side of the river from his garden. Not too high, you know, about as tall as the top of your house off the ground. Look I know you're going to hate me for this, but I can't help telling you. See, he's got this little bit of water in the top part of his garden, kind of a little puddle in the middle of his flowers. Well, when you've got eyes as good as mine (and my, have I got good eyes!) you can't help noticing all those fat goldy-red fish zonking about in that little bit of water. Oh Gaia!, you've got to understand, I mean, they're fish aren't they? I mean, I eat fish don't I?

The other morning, I'm afraid I just had to have a closer look at those little goldie numbers, just curious, don't you know. Well, to be honest, hungry actually. I mean, be fair, if you had a choice between lying in bed and having your food put into your mouth for you, or having to zonk about all over the place just to find a biscuit, what would *you* do? Got it? Yep! I ate them! Very nice too. I just stood there looking down at the water, and the silly fish just lay there looking up at me, and they seemed to be saying, 'Well, look at us. Look how well fed we are. Look at how fat we are.'

What a cheek. Here's me, as thin as a pole, and they're just goggling at me. So, a quick look to make sure that there are no hoomans about, none of those noisy black and white jobs with brushy tails that make a lot of woofy noises and tear about like maniacs either, and I'm stabbing down into the water. Oh Gaia, a piece of cake - well, fish actually. A nice fat golden fish. Lift it out of the water, give it a little flick in the air to turn the head towards my beak, and down it goes. Why head first? Come on! Ever tried to push a Christmas tree through a door with the roots first? I mean, fish might have a tiny end, but the fins stick out the wrong way, and those little flaps at the sides of their heads might get stuck in my gullet, and I don't like choking any more than you do.

'Oh Herbie', I hear you say, 'how could you do such a thing?' Natural, that's the word. I'm not so clever as owls, but I know a few choice words; one that comes to mind is *opportunist*.

What else can I tell you? Oh dear... you want to know about my love life? This is a bit embarrassing really. I mean, I know you hoomans make your nests in houses and things, and the lady hoomans have baby hoomans at home or in those big hospital nests with lots of babies in them. I know you're going to think this is a bit silly, but we herons have our babies in the tops of trees!

There, I said it, you can laugh now. 'You mean to say that you great big herons have babies in the tops of trees? He-he-he-he-he.' Hey watch it. That laughter sounded a bit like birdsong... hmmm... interesting that. Yes, we *do* make our nests in the tops of high trees if possible, and because we are big birds, I've got to confess that we make BIG nests. In fact, some of the biggest nests you can imagine. One of you could almost curl up in the nest I built last year. Mind you, no electric blankets or duvets I'm afraid, we're not into that kind of thing. Of course, there are some herons that make nests in reeds and even on cliff edges, but for most of us, it's a nice lofty tree perch or nothing.

Can you keep another secret? You can? Okay, well, cop this one. We heron's aren't afraid of much. I mean, we're pretty scary really, being big and all, and wouldn't you be a little scared if there was a forty-foot high hooman in your area who walked about with a twenty-foot sword on the front of his face instead of a nose? Sure you would. But here's the secret bit: there's actually an awful lot down there to be scared of if you happen to be a little bit of pale grey fluff called a baby heron. You've got no idea how many creatures there are down there that feel the same way about baby herons as I do about goldfish - know what I mean?

Well, it's like this, it's not hard to work it out. Take foxes for example, not that I've got anything against foxes really, but they do have a nasty habit of sticking their wet noses in just where you don't want them. I mean, they're so clever you know, got a sense of smell like noses are going out of business. No wonder they smell so bad... whoops; where was I? Oh yes... well, there's one thing a crafty fox can't do that I can. Got it? Yep, they can't fly - harrrrrrrrrrrr! Now it's my turn to laugh. Yep, foxes can't fly. So we build our nests high up just 'cos they can't fly up there, see?

Mind you, foxes are the least of our worries. There are animals on the ground down there, hungry things that can't fly, but Gaia, can they climb! I mean, there are weasels and stoats for starters. Tough little critters, bobbing about like little fur sticks on a string, all red and brown and white. Not my favourite colours, brown and red, to be honest. Well, even they can't get up as high as we are, right at the tops of the most lofty trees we can find.

Once a year, often before those green flappy leaves sprout all over the branches of the trees, we get going on the hunt for dead twigs and small branches - usually plenty about after all those winter winds have finished smashing things up. You've got to have a good head for heights, and a very strong beak and balancing legs too. Imagine doing some Lego about sixty feet up a tree that feels as though it's got a minor earthquake shaking it. That's what it's like up there. Anyway, somehow, we get the sticks to slot into each other. Pretty hard that, just with a long bill and a spare foot - none of these big bundles of pink wavy things that you hoomans build things with - what do you call them? Fingers... lucky you.

I expect you might be wondering how we get a lady heron to make a nest with us? Well, even if you don't, it's always a bit of a worry for me! Usually, we males arrive first at the tree tops where we nest. If I can remember where I left it, I like to work on the nest I used last year. I know, I know, 'Herbie, you're lazy' you might say. Hey, well come on now, wouldn't *you* choose a house half built to set up home in rather than start again from scratch?

A little time after we guys arrive, the arguments start. Not that we actually get rough or anything like that, but we do a lot of shouting, and give each other a lot of nasty looks, and lift our long black crests up in the air and flap our wings. It's our way of telling another guy to clear off. I mean, well, some of these guys are so lazy, can't be bothered to build a nest of their own, and the first-timers are the worst. They just seem to hate doing any work for themselves. Now me, I was never like that: huaaaark - just kidding!

When the lady herons turn up, it gets a bit confusing. Why? Because they look the same as us guys of course! Ah well, I won't bore you with how we work that out, but somehow we do. Oh dear, I don't know how to say this, but we only have a partner for a year at a time. Last year, Henrietta was my partner, and we raised three nice healthy young ones. She liked the way I croaked and flapped, and well... one thing led to another and before we knew where we were, there she was sitting on three eggs. I hate all that sitting about myself, but a guy has to do his bit too, so we take it in turns to keep the eggs warm. Got to do that you know, no electric blankets, remember? Oh Gaia, once those little fluffy babies get going the work really starts. I mean, I hope you guys didn't spend the whole day yelling for food when you were babies, but our little ones did! Personally, I couldn't wait to see the little darlings hop off the nest and fly. Oooo, all that hard work. Makes my feathers droop, just thinking about it.

How do we know how to fly? Easy, we practice! The young ones spend a lot of time just standing there and flapping. I mean, if your mum and dad stopped feeding you in bed, you'd get up and walk to the kitchen wouldn't you? Well, in our case, the kitchen isn't at the top of a tree so it's fly or starve. Watching our young ones fly for the first time is a hoot, if you follow my owl talk! I mean, there's a lot of pranging and crashing about, but they get the hang of it pretty fast. Even funnier is watching the chicks fishing for the first time. Nine times out of ten they miss the fish!

Ah well, as I croaked before, it's all a matter of practice. We grown-ups usually clear off by the summer. This is a good time to see us herons. We sometimes get in big groups and stand about dreaming. Not much *kraaaking* at all, just standing there in groups of three, or much more. A friend of mine in Cumbria told me that he often stands with as many as twenty other herons, you know, just standing there, looking dopey, I guess, but it makes a nice change from all that family stuff.

I'd better get moving soon, those fish are waiting! Winter is sometimes tough for us herons. If the frost gets too bad, we have a hard time finding food, and I'm sorry to say that a few of us starve and flutter off to bird-heaven. Now you're going to find this hard as well, but to be honest, you hoomans are a pain in the fluff sometimes. I mean do you really *have* to put all those long wires on those big poles. I knew a mate of mine who broke his neck on one. Flew straight into it - couldn't see it you see...

And here's another grumble *(krrrreeeak,* actually*)*, I *do* wish you hoomans who go along our water places with those long fishing sticks and thin lines would stop leaving those lines lying about. They make the most awful mess if we get entangled in them. I mean, *we* don't leave our beaks lying all over the place now do we? Ah well, enough of the grumbling. Maybe you can understand why we birds are a bit shy of hoomans. If you ever come along my way, do give me a wave.

Don't come too close, 'cos I'll only fly off. Just keep a nice distance between you and me and honestly, I don't mind if you stare one bit! I do a lot of staring myself.

And if you don't see me on the ground, chances are that one of these days, you'll look up, and there I'll be, drifting or flapping lazily by, and if you really want to see me personally, well, you'll have to take a boat trip down the River Dart from Totnes to Dartmouth in the spring. Just ask the guide to point us out, we'll be there in our nests, right in the tops of the trees, on the left hand side as you go down-river, okay?

Ho-hum! time to go, nice talking to you.

Byeeeeeeeeeeeeeeeeeeee.

Serena the Mute Swan

## Serena the Mute Swan

Well hello! Quite a surprise to be asked to talk to you hoomans! To be perfectly honest, I don't usually talk much. I can't quite see the point. When you are snowy white and as big as I am, you don't need to talk much. Most birds just get out of the way. I can't imagine you trying to talk a big truck into stopping for you, not much point is there? Better to get out of the way. That's why your big trucks don't talk much either, I guess.

Some birds would be offended at being called 'mute', but it doesn't bother us mute swans. We have cousins called whooper swans and trumpeter swans, and you can just imagine what we think about that. *Undignified*, I hiss it. All that whooping and trumpeting, no decorum if you ask me! But then, I guess they have their reasons for being so noisy. You see, they do a lot more long-distance flying than us mute swans, so I think they talk a lot to keep in touch with each other, kind of in-flight entertainment perhaps?

What's a mute? Well, do any of you play the violin or a trumpet or trombone? Oh, well if you did, you'd know that you can put a little something on the strings of your violin to make it play quieter, or put a piece of tubular stuff in your trumpet to make it sound softer. These things are called mutes. Since we are so quiet, we are called mute swans. Have you got that all right? Good!

You'd find it awfully hard to speak mute swan. We have so many hissing *sksheeeeetkts* and *skrrshweeeers*! It's not the easiest of languages to copy, unless you like to pretend to be a steam engine getting cross!

I hear that you've been talking to Herbie. He's a big bird too, though not really as big as we are. Put Herbie on some bird scales and it's okay, but put one of us on some, and you'd soon hear the scales say, 'one at a time please'.

Well, how heavy is that? Next time you go shopping with your mum or dad, ask them to let you hold a couple of baskets of groceries when they are full of food, and you'd get some idea of how heavy I am. Being that heavy has its drawbacks, I must confess. You see, we like to fly too, and for many of the same reasons as Herbie does. The problem is one of getting all that weight into the air. Ever been to an airport? You have? Well, ever noticed that little aeroplanes don't need much  runway to take off from? Those big jets, what do you call them? *Jumbos?* Why is that? I thought they were elephants! Now they need a *lot* of runway to get into the air. I'm sure you are getting the idea. We mute swans are the birdie jumbos! We need a run of more than a hundred metres to get into the air, so don't expect me to drop into your goldfish pond for a chat, because I won't! It's hard taking off. We start flapping our wings, and they make a lot of noise on the surface of the water. At the same time, we use our big paddle feet, and run with them to give us an extra push forwards.

Unlike Herbie, we fly with our necks stretched out straight. I really can't imagine how Herbie manages to fly with his neck all bent and crooked like that, but everyone to their own taste. In my swanny mind it's more elegant to fly with a straight neck, but I don't want you to think that I'm a snob, even if I am. Well, just a little perhaps! Where was I? Oh yes, taking off. Now when we swans get into the air - you've got to hand it to us - we are just beautiful. Great big deep wing beats, and heaps of lovely whistling sounds from our wing tip feathers. To be honest, it's a bit embarrassing as to just how *much* noise our wings make. If you could just hear us, you really would wonder why we are called mute swans!

Mind you, when we do fly long distances, or in those big woolly grey mists we seem to get from time to time, it's comforting to hear those noises from the other swans in the flight, sort of helps us to know where each of us is if you know what I mean. I think we look wonderful in the air, though I've got to confess that we are not very good at turning corners in flight, we're just not built for all that dodging and weaving that some birds do. Why should we anyway? I mean, we are so big that we don't need to turn. Any seagull in our flight path knows what to do - get out of the way!

I have to confess that nice bird though he is, we don't have an awful lot in common with Herbie the heron. I'd hate to have breath that smelt of fish, like his does. We mute swans are vegetarians, can't stand the taste of anything else. Yes, sometimes we might accidentally swallow an insect or two in the grasses and weeds that we like to eat, but insects give me indigestion, so I tend to avoid them. Hmmmmmmm, we don't eat in the most, well, how shall I put it, *elegant* of fashions!

The chances are that if you come along when I'm eating, you won't be able to see my head at all. Why? (Herbie warned me that you ask a lot of questions!) Well, we just tip up our tails and turn upside down in the water you see! The best vegetation in the water is *under* the water, so we don't have much choice in the matter. It may seem odd that such big birds eat such little things as blades of water grasses and weeds, but where I live, there is a lot of it about and, oh Gaia, my dears, we need a lot of food to keep us going.

Of course, we are not opposed to eating things on the surface as well, but to be honest, the sweetest and nicest things to eat are on the bottom of streams, rivers and lakes. So there it is, up-tails all! Now when it comes to actually *seeing* mute swans, well, you can't really miss us, now can you? We are so lovely and white you see, and so big! Being so big makes it easier for us swans. Not much frightens us either, so we don't have to bother about being hidden or anything like that. We don't need to wear special feathers to disguise us. Now what's the word? Ah yes, to *camouflage* us. No my dears, we don't need that!

Well, I warned you that we swans don't have much in common with Herbie. When it comes to partners, I have to confess that herons have got me puzzled. We swans get married for life you see. I'm too lazy to get divorced. I couldn't stand the insecurity, but each to their own, I say! I've been with my partner Sidney, for over ten years, and we've had dozens of babies together. Each year we find a nice quiet spot on the river bank, snuggled up in a very plush and lush bunch of tall reeds, and build the biggest nest you can possibly imagine, my dears! You could *definitely* curl up in one of our nests, and you'd be very snug and comfortable too.

The bottom is a bed base of soft rushes and reeds, and we line the inside with soft feathers (mostly plucked from my own chest as a matter of fact). Lovely and fluffy and silky soft and warm. Nice! I can't be exact in telling you how many babies we have each year, but I'd be letting the side down if I had less than five eggs to look after.

Right from the start, our babies look like swans, but coloured grey, and thank goodness, they can feed themselves straight away. I don't even have to show them how to swim! Sidney is such a sweetie whilst I'm sitting on the eggs. He just floats about a lot, looking fierce. To tell you the truth, he doesn't just *look* fierce during those few weeks, he *is* fierce! Don't be so silly as to get too close to have a peek at my nest. You'll just make him cross, that's all. He'll get those big wings all streched up and tight, and he'll surge towards you with those great big paddle-feet pushing him through the water. Then he'll... well... what can I say... hiss at you! And if you are silly enough to meet him on the land at that time, you'd better beat a quick retreat, and I mean quick. He's got a swan-belt in karate, and those wings of his are pretty tough, so don't be silly dears. Keep your distance.

Now don't go getting all offended and upset at Sidney's behaviour. He's just doing his job you know. Baby swans are really quite small, and those nasty foxes and weasels and things wouldn't think twice about gobbling down one of my young ones. So there it is. And if you were a bird like a seagull, or a crow, and you liked omelettes as much as they do, you'd be the first to understand why Sidney hangs about looking like a big white Rambo, and why we both cover the eggs with leaves when we are off the nest; now wouldn't you? I knew you'd understand. Thank you dearies!

It's a shame that our babies are so grey when young. I've always thought that our young ones let the side down a bit. But, thank Gaia, they are grey because they are less obvious when wearing that colour. Once they get big enough, they lose all those grey feathers and grow nice respectable white ones just like us. Oh what a tough time that is, when we change our feathers each year. It's all right for you hoomans, you can just change your clothes all the time, and since you don't fly, you don't need your clothes to get you into the air, but we do, you see.

So for several weeks we get to look a bit scruffy and lose a lot of our feathers. In fact, though I wouldn't want this gossiped about, we actually can't fly at all whilst we change our feathers, which makes things just a little bit awkward. Sidney and I have an arrangement. He changes his feathers at a different time from me. It's safer that way. Always nice to have a few of us who can get into the air. Of course, we do take precautions at this time of the year. You'll be able to see just heaps and heaps of us together when we *moult*. Hmmmmmmmm, not the nicest sounding word, but it's your fault. You hoomans thought of that word to describe when we change our feathers. If I had any choice, I'd call this *skrsheee* - but I doubt if that would mean much to you!

I don't know if you've noticed this, but we swans don't mind you hoomans much. In fact some of my best friends are hoomans! I mean, you make such lovely yummy things to eat. I have to say that I like the bread best. Not awfully fond of beefburgers or chips! It's awfully nice when you little darlings come along to the river and throw us some bread to eat. It does save me a lot of neck-stretching and, to be honest, it's also a nice change to eat something the right way up!

I'd better go now. I really must glide off and find a nice bit of river bottom to stick my beak into. By the way, in case you feel uncertain about telling Sidney and me apart, he's the one with the biggest nobbly black bump on his bill, and he's the one who gets a bit puffy with his wings when he gets cross, remember? And please don't get upset if you see some of us with little plastic rings on our legs, we don't mind at all. Most of us belong to a great big family in special areas, and there are nice hoomans who want to find out things about us. Since we look very much alike in a big group, it must be awfully helpful to be able to see the little labels on our legs!

Oh dear, look who's waiting to talk to you, one of those silly water birds that really do irritate me, if you don't mind my saying so. I don't envy you listening to his babble and burble. Good luck to you!

It's been awfully nice talking to you. Do drop by and see

me sometime, but not when I'm nesting, that's not a good time for a chat. I'm very busy then, and Sidney will only get all white and bothered. Bye dears!

Clive the Coot

## Clive the Coot

Kut! Kut! Pskoot... what? Oh man... I mean..., I forgot to use the cool translator thing... whoops... sorry man... oh man... wow... cool! Yeah, well now... like, oh man... ya know... hi and things!

Glad that snobby Serena swan has cleared off, I mean, oh man, what a snooty bird. Always looking down her beak at you, and wow, I mean, that husband of hers! G-A-I-A, what a bad tempered kind of dude. Not cool like us coots, man.

'S the same every autumn, I mean, like we get together in our big flocks for the winter, ya know, big coot fest time. Like one of your cool pop fests... yeah! hundreds of us like fooling and cooling around, great fun actually. Cool to chase each other's tails man, might seem rude to you, but nothing more fun than flashing them black tail feathers at another cool dude. Makes 'em kinda wild.

While we're having a cool time tearing about like... well, like coots, those swans just slowpoke around looking like they own the place. No sense of humour, ya know. Nothing more un-cool than a swanny bunch of swans in winter. To us coots, racing each other round the lake is great, I mean, well ya don't get speeding tickets if you're a coot, in fact if ya don't break the speed limit, you're not a cool coot at all.

Here, while I'm on the subject, how come you hoomans are so rude about us? I mean, that expression you lot 'ave, 'bald as a coot', well, I mean, hey, that's not very nice is it? We can't 'elp 'aving a big white bald patch on our bills, ya know. A big white nobbly bit where you dudes perch your glasses if you wear specs? Well, I mean to say, if you were pretty black all over like us coots, a bit of white breaks the monotony a bit, helps to make faces with if you follow my meaning.

And hey, if you want to see something *really* cool, I mean, just take a look at our eyes. Oh man, red eyes, yeah. Red eyes man. Not when we're young like, we get red eyes when we get grown up, kinda suits the image ya know.

In a way, we wear kinda uniforms, like you dudes do when you're in the police force or when you goes to parties in them flashy suits, DJs ya know? Cool!

Oh man, it's cool being a coot. I mean like there's so many of us, yeah, all over the place. No bit of water is too small to have a good time in, not snobbish like them swans I mean, man, if your fish pond was as big as your lawn and you had some real cool reeds growing around, well, man oh man, I'd be there like a shot and so would half a dozen of my buddies too.

It's the nosh, you see. Nothing much we won't get our fun out of eating. You name it; grasses, weeds, insects, little shrimps... yeah, anything goes in the coot cafe! Okay, okay, I know we bash each other up a lot, but it's only fun ya know, like it's the rule here. I mean, everybody thinks he's the top coot and well, I don't like that really. I mean everyone should know that me, Clive, is the top coot. And all the coot chicks, man oh man, are they cool. I mean, them girls is as rough as guys. I got bashed up by one yesterday. Oh wow, was she rough, came at me like a maniac she did, wings flapping like crazy, threw herself back and kicked at me like a great coot-kick-boxer. Oh man, and those wild eyes. Don't tell my mates, but I beat a hasty retreat, too hot to handle she was. So I just turned tail and flicked a few black tail wags at her, and I made sure she remembered my voice too. Nobody can do the cute *koot*! better than Clive here. Cool. Hey, I mean, it's no good asking me to 'give you five', but I'm cool with four, yeah! Four toes slapping mine, best way to say hi, that I know.

That cool she-coot that beat me up yesterday, I'd better remember her, she's cool, man. I'd like to date her next spring, but I don't know, she might not stay around to get some coot kids on the go.

See, we just hang around for the winter fest, safety in numbers, man. I mean, there's some real tykes round here. If it's not those 'orrible harriers that come across the water like a rocket going sideways, ripping us poor coots to shreds and gobbling us up, it's those blinkin' sparrowhawks. Same tactics: sneak along the reeds and dive along the surface. Next thing you know, you're gone man. Not cool that. So we stays in big bunches so as to keep 'em confused ya know.

And don't expect us to come on land for 'walkies' on our own either - that's not cool man. I mean, them foxes, and even rats take a lot of pleasure in scaring us half to death, so we keep in big gangs see, lots of us on the lookout, just in case, even take it in turns on guard. Got to do a good job mind. We got real cross with Chris coot last week, 'cos he didn't yell out when a fox came by to complain about our coot fest on his patch, oh man, that fox ate two of us before Chris even said *kut*, oh man, thick as a log is Chris. Nobody's going to put *him* on watch again.

Come the spring, things get kinda hot, if you know what I mean. I mean, man, we can't all nest in this place, too many of us. I mean, those young coot kids eat an awful lot and we need some space of our own to keep the nosh going for 'em. And another thing, too many coot guys for my liking, everyone wants to date a cool coot lady. So we have to get a bit tough ya know. That's what's so good about the winter fest, great time to practice a few whooshing rushes and the odd toe kick - helps to keep the voice in good order too.

Now I've got a great voice. I can *kut*! like you wouldn't believe and hey, don't try to tell *me* to shut up after dark 'cos I won't, so there. You can fight just as well in the dark, I assure you. Hey! They can't see you coming in the dark, see, I mean, man, I'm blacker than the night!

Once I've got a nice missus to fool around with, it's straight down to business, if ya know what I mean. Find a nice cool flat patch of reeds, or a nice big slurpy bit of mud-bank, snugged up under a big sleepy willow, and we're off.

Man, how my beak aches! I mean, you'd get tired too if you had to carry all those bits of rushes and twigs to get the nest base done, and build a nice big cup to put the eggs in, hey man, 'cause we've got to build up the sides. Uncool to let the eggs roll out, see. Last year, I made three hundred and twenty seven trips with bits of this and that for the new nest. I was plum cooted out by the end of it and hey, we guys can't clear off and have a rest ya know, got to do our bit in looking after those eggs, they need my warm fluffy bottom to get the chicks to hatch as well as the missus. Hey, remember the coot fest? Well, cool, I mean, one of my favourite tricks is to do a bit of drumming on the nest platform... oh great! Get it nice and flat and wet... and then stomp up and down with my big feet, what a great noise - *pittapattapittapatta!* I don't like confessing this, but we coots can't swim as well as those snooty swans or those busybody ducks. I mean, man oh man, what big feet they've got, and they've got their toes filled in too with bits of flaps like flippers. I mean we don't have webbed feet at all, we're not on the web see - hooo arrr! What a joke... not on the web... got it? Mind you, speaking for us coots, I reckon we've got cool feet, I mean... man, we *have* got little bits of webbing on each toe, helps to stop us from getting bogged down in the mud - wooo hoooo! Another joke - bogged down! Get it? Wow!

Hey, it's tough being a smallish water bird, I mean us coots are small enough to fit into your Corn Flakes packet, man! Try stuffing Herbie, or that snooty Serena, into your Coco Pops packet. Wow, what a mess of the packet you'd make. Mind you, we're a bit bigger than moorhens, but who cares about moorhens? I mean, hey, they might have nice coloured beaks and they might look a lot like us from the back, but well, to be honest... they are a bit too slim and namby-pamby for the likes of me. I prefer the image of being a little on the plump side myself - cool!

Hey, don't get the idea that we coots have an easy time rearing the little ones. I mean, man, we have so many. My missus and me had thirteen last year. No silly, not all at once, we had two goes, see, best year we had. The previous year we tried twice, well, another missus and me did, but we made a silly mistake, see, built the nest too close to the water, and it, well, kinda rained a lot, and hey, the water came up and washed the nest away. I mean, man, how stupid can you get... I'd have kicked myself if I could but I couldn't so we just started all over again... and the same thing happened again. I realise that was un-cool - I mean, man, it's our duty to make little coots every year or else we'd get nowehere would we? And there's nothing more boring than a winter coot fest with only six coots there, know what I mean?

Hey, don't expect me to talk about flying - us coots don't do a lot of that. Mind you, my cool coot pal Colin, well man, *he's* been up to three hundred metres, yep, just flew up and showed us how to do it. Mind you, I'm a bit fed up with Colin, the last time he did that we never saw him again, just cleared off without saying *kutbye*. What a cheek - I mean how could he? Real un-cool if you ask me.

Hey, well, I've got to go over there and bash up that gang of noisy guys. I mean, here I am trying to talk to you, and they keep flashing their tails at me. What a face! Sorry I can't stay longer. I'm off, time to get tough.

Oi! You lot... pack that up... hey! I'm *kutting* to you... yes, you... oh really? Like to look at my feet in your face, eh? Okay, well, cool... get a load of this then... *woooossh-hhh-hhhhh... kut... kut... kut... kut...*

Mavis the Mallard

## Mavis the Mallard

Oh no... not really? Must I? Really? Now? I have to talk now? It's my turn? Oh! Whatever can I say? Mmmm... I know... whenever you see us mallards out and about, we seem to be doing nothing but talking, but I'm not used to talking to you hoomans. I'm far too shy, you see. Oh, I know why you are confused, you think I'm one of those brown ducks that swims on the farm pond or in those fancy lakes where you play in the park? Well, I can understand now... hmmmm. Yes, some of those brown ducks *are* mallards like me, but many of them are not.

Hmmm? Oh, well you see, you hoomans have been eating us for thousands of years and you have bred your own special brown ducks for pets, though if you don't mind my saying so, it's a funny kind of pet when you fatten them up and then eat them. Ah well, I've never been able to understand you hoomans!

Come to think of it, not only do you hoomans eat us by the thousands each year, just about everything else that likes meat does too. It's a wonder that there are any of us left! It's a jolly good thing that we have such a lot of babies, otherwise I shudder my lovely brown feathers to think of the consequences! Now, I do love my feathers, such a lovely mixture of browns and soft greys and may I say that I doubt if any bird has a more wonderful set of purple feathers on their wings than I have.

Many of us ducks have these lovely coloured feathers on our wings. I guess it's a sort of badge that shows others who we are. In the autumn, we lose a lot of feathers to grow some new ones and our husbands lose theirs too, and for a while the men-ducks really look like us ladies. Worse still, other brown ducks look like us as well. So it's a jolly good thing to have those lovely coloured flashes on our shoulders. Stops a lot of very embarrassing moments, I can assure you.

I saw you talking to that unspeakable Clive the coot. What a rude bird! Did he show off a lot? I'll bet he did. He and his kind are always showing off. Most of them even think they can dive! I'm not going to tell duck-fibs. We mallards aren't very good at diving, and neither are coots. So there. Our babies are a different matter. Even I have to confess that baby coots and baby mallards are actually quite good at diving, but we adults don't stay down for long. In fact, neither grown-up coots nor mallards stay under water for much longer than it takes you to read this sentence, and that's a fact!

Serena the swan and I have quite a few things in common. We eat our meals mainly under the surface of the water. In fact, I see more of Serena dabbling upside down than I do sitting the right way up! Of course, she can eat her supper in deeper water than I can, she has such a long neck, but then swans are always sticking their necks out, like to be at least six beaks above the rest of us poor water birds. Except Herbie. Well, *he* is miles in the air, which is probably why he's such a dreamer.

Have I talked too much? So sorry, oh, you'd like to know a little more? How nice of you! Talking of talking, which is to say quacking of quacking, we lady mallards actually talk more than our male partners! Now isn't that nice! I mean, most lady birds (that's *female birds*, dear things, *not* those lovely red beetles with the black spots!) hardly talk at all. Why, I know several lady blackbirds who hardly ever say a word, can't get a word in beak-ways what with their noisy husbands, warbling and trilling all over the place!

By the way, quacking about diving, I expect some of you awfully clever hoomans have noticed that some of my duck cousins are wonderful divers. On the lake where I live, there are several cousins who dive most frightfully well, especially those black and white ducks with little black tuffts on their heads... what are they called, dear ones? Why, tufted ducks of course! You hoomans are so clever with your names, so clever, I mean what else *would* you call a black and white duck with a tuft on its head but tufted duck? But I do wish you would be careful with some of your names for us, I mean, another cousin of mine has daddy ducks with lovely nut brown heads and pale grey bodies. Well, I mean, they dive wonderfully too but you don't call them brown headed ducks... you call them pochards. Now that really is very silly, isn't it? No wonder you have such a hard time remembering all our names!

Here's a little trick to help you know which of us ducks feeds on the surface and which does not. Diving ducks have tails just like me, but they keep their tails flat against the smooth surface of the water. Why there are a few who actually keep their tails just *under* the water! So neat, so thoughtful, they just tip up, and slide smartly under the water and if they had a tail that was lifted out of the water like mine, surely it would make the dive that bit harder, no?

Now, us surface ducks keep our tails bobbed up at the back of our bodies, such a nice feeling to waggle it about sometimes, you know up and down and from side to side and when we tip up and stick our head into the water, it's so cute to have a nice long tail sticking up to keep us in balance.

Now I don't want you to think that I'm boastful, or anything like that, but I'll bet you've had a lot of talk from the others about how well they fly? Well, they *would*, wouldn't they? I mean, if I didn't love the colour green so much and if our husbands didn't have such *sexy* shining green heads, I would say that the others were *green* with envy at how well we mallards can fly!

Oh, you silly billy hoomans! Why on Gaia do you say funny things like *fly straight as an arrow*? What you *should* say is *fly as straight as a mallard*! Once we mallards are in the air, we really do fly so lovely and straight and if you are lucky enough to see a whole lot of us high in the air, you may be able to see what a beautiful shape we make as we go long distance! Put your two fingers apart and hold  them up in the air, now turn them sideways, you will see that you have made a lovely 'V'. Nice eh? We often fly in 'V' patterns, like most of our cousins, and even distant cousins like geese and swans.

Why? Oh my dear ones, it's hard to fly long distance without getting tired! So much wind up there, so much thick air to fly through, makes my feathers shake just thinking about how thick air is when you are trying to move fast through it. When we fly in a 'V' the duck at the front decides where we are going, and the ones on either side of the 'V' get some of the wind taken away by the leader's body and beating wings... mmm... so nice! Then we change places and some other duck goes to the front to give the previous leader a rest. Aren't we *clever*?

When the spring comes, those nasty frosts go away, the primroses and violets start to put their delightful yellow or dark-blue flowers all over the place - oh my, what a lovely smell! Well, that's the time to start to think about... well... you can guess surely? Hmmmmmm? Well, yes, making baby ducks of course! Now this is *really* embarrassing... makes me blush... except that I can't turn red! There are so many hunky sexy daddy mallards about in the spring, far more than us ladies. I've quacked several letters of complaint to Mother Gaia about this, but she just doesn't seem to want to answer them.

So my dears, I'm afraid to confess that we lady mallards often date several daddy ones at once. Well, that's not quite true, I mean those delicious dancing daddy mallards make such wonderful shapes with their sheen-green heads bobbing up and down, heaps of them at once, I mean, what's a girl to do?

Yes, we do get married for the season, but I'm afraid the glitter of a ducky engagement ring doesn't put those silly boys off. And if you think a wedding ring would stop them from chasing us married mallards about, forget it! In fact, to be honest, it only makes them worse!

Last year I had a date with a most handsome mallard drake... my what a green noddle he had! We got married and built a super nest, lots of nice reeds and grasses lined with my best and softest chest feathers. I laid ten eggs, but oh my dears, I'm not at all sure that he was the father of all those cute little ducklings!

I couldn't help myself you see, such a lot of lush ducks about, so keen to please me and join in the fun. Oh dear, I am getting bold, no wonder we lady mallards have such a bad reputation! Mind you, I'm sorry to say that there are more than a few of those cheeky males that won't take *quack* for a 'no'! To be honest, we ladies sometimes don't have any choice in the matter, so there it is. Most likely at least half of my ducklings last year weren't Maurice mallard's, but probably Mick's and Mervyn's as well. Please don't tell Maurice if you see him, he's so pompous and proud, it might hurt his feelings!

Hurt his feelings? What am I saying? I'm sorry to say that after he's done his fancy dancing dates with me and helped a bit with the nest, he just sits around for a couple of weeks and, well... just sits. Once the dear little ones chip their way out of the eggs, does he paddle over and say, 'oh, well done, can I lend a hand?' Does he *quack*! My dears he just hops it! Well, if he could hop he would. In fact I'm sorry to say that as soon as our little dear ducklings were skipping through the water behind me, he was off canoodling with that awful Mona mallard. For all I know, some of her ducklings were little Maurice's babies as well. Ah well, such is life.

Can I stop now? Oh really? *Must* I? Oh all right, I guess it's my own fault, talking about mallard marriages and things. Yes, yes, I agree that one of us birds should tell you hoomans exactly how we make little baby birds. Well, take us mallards for example. During those warm spring months, when we are busy making nests and our husbands are being so attentive, you hoomans may have noticed one of the male mallards come up behind us and push our heads under the water and climb up onto the backs of our bodies? It's a jolly good thing that we can hold our breath!

Well, I know it looks as though they are trying to drown us, but actually it's far nicer than that. Deep inside us lady mallards, there are some eggs waiting to come out with little specks inside the yolks. The trouble is that we lady mallards can't make those specks grow on our own. What we need is to have some little tiny wiggly things inside us (I believe you hoomans call them *sperms*) to go and find those eggs and make them change, so that a baby can start to grow. So what Maurice did last year was to get on top of my back, stretch my neck out, pushing down on me at the same time. I lifted my tail and uncovered the little hole that is the place where I lay my eggs from. He squirted a little milky liquid onto the underneath of his tail and tipped it under my tail and gently wiped the fluid onto that little hole that I have. The little wiggly things find their way inside me and swim to find an egg. Once they find one, they swim right inside and join up with the little bit I keep there just for that wiggly thing to join. Once joined, they start to make lots and lots of things happen there - bones, muscles, and even eyes, a brain and heart grow quickly - and a little duck is made in each egg. Every egg that is visited by a little wiggly thing from Maurice is now fertilised and a little duckling can grow.

There, now I've told you. All birds make babies that way, except birds like Serena swan, and our geese cousins. The daddy swans and geese actually have a long piece of skin between their legs, that is shaped like a piece of straw. With this they can actually put the piece of skin inside their partners and squirt the little wiggly sperms straight inside. Clever that, wonder why we ducks don't?

Well, dear ones, I have a 'V' to catch. Plenty of us mallards about, so you can hardly miss us now can you? Bye, and thanks for listening!

Basil the Black Headed Gull

## Basil the Black Headed Gull

H-how do! Sorry about that, but I've got a bit of a stutter. Sometimes I just can't seem to g-get the w-words out right. Seems to me that w-we birds have it a bit r-rough, trying to talk with such long b-beaks. You'll 'ave to j-just go along w-with me that's all, c-can't help it see. I've got no idea w-what I'm doin' here with all these fresh w-water birds. I'm a s-s-sea bird myself! Well, actually that's n-not quite true - *used* to be a s-s-sea bird... b-but we've 'ad such a great time spreading our w-wings in the country that you'll see one of us j-just about everywhere nowa-days. It's all a matter of bein' able to eat most anythin' see... t-take me for example... I'll eat j-just about anything. I love all that stuff you h-hoomans leave lying about, spe-cially those great g-garbage tips you 'ave... they're great for us g-gulls!

Speaking p-personal like, I like it when you come to Scarborough for your h-holidays and feed us gulls on t'-beach. Last summer, I got so fat on all those nice g-greasy chips and s-sandwiches you left around, that I 'ad a job taking off again sometimes. I 'ave some m-mates 'oo live near York an' they get a right good bit of feeding in't late s-summer when you h-hoomans do that funny thing with those big noisy machines in the farm fields. I mean, w-what do you d-do that for?

I can't believe what my mates say, that you turn all that soil over just to f-feed us gulls. That can't be right surely? Anyway, they told me that all they 'ave to d-do is just fly behind them big machines and p-pounce down on the fat-test worms in Yorkshire. Lucky beggars, I say! Mind you, we g-gulls do our best to entertain you. Last summer I tried some right f-fancy tricks of f-flying, ya know, spun round in mid-air like a spinning top and even got the 'ang of t-taking a corned-beef sandwich up-s-side down, got a round of applause d-did that and one of you hoomans t-took my picture doin' it. I was that proud, ooo-arr!

In t'winter, the oddest thing 'appens to us black headed-gulls, c-can't quite work out why it does, b-but we seem to lose our whole heads, j-just the black feathers, like. We just seem to keep a little bit of black stuff, right where our ears are, so you'd probably n-never guess we was black-headed g-gulls at all!

Well, we 'ave to ch-change our feathers each year like. You've got no idea what a battering our f-feathers get just f-flying about. If you look up at us flying in August you can s-sometimes see our wing feathers, all tatty and torn. Quite a problem that, makes it hard to do the fancy s-stuff I like to do! So we get together in big groups, and I m-mean *big* groups and change our feathers for new ones. The b-black head starts to grow back after Christmas, just in time for some canoodling in the spring.

Gulls are p-pretty smart, you know. You hoomans don't seem to eat your food in as m-many different ways as we do. I mean, we can pounce and stab, and winkle things out of little spaces, and catch things in the air as well. I b-bet you can't do that - catch things in the air I mean. Some of my gull c-cousins even stomp about with their feet to bring worms up to eat, you know, pretending to be rain-drops. Smart, eh? Now I *love* worms, got to be honest about that.

Come t'spring, we stay in big bunches to make our nests. Me, I like to find a nice big stretch of water with plenty of reeds or little t-trees around to give us a little p-privacy like, well, p-privacy from interfering animals that is. Such a worry, too many hungry animals about in t'spring for m-my liking.

Hey, I hope you hoomans don't do as much thieving and

p-pinching as we do when you build your nests. It's a f-full time job keeping an eye on the nest. Take one second to tickle and clean a few dirty feathers and some other g-gull has taken half your house away - not v-very nice that! Got to confess, I do it myself too, you know, wait till one of 'em is busy, and wing over and nick a few twigs.

I suppose it's all a m-matter of being a b-bit over-crowded like, next door neighbour being only a couple of flaps away makes it real t-tempting. Sometimes, we get unwelcome visitors, mates of mine have otters on the scene. Bad news, otters. Can't th-think why they can't stick to fishing, but they do have a nasty habit of t-taking the odd little dappled gull chick. Well, I m-m-m-mean... 'ow could they?

If they do come by we get in a right f-flap and rush up into a tower of b-birds, up in the sky, rising and falling, like white yo-yos on a string, yelling and screaming, like. Jolly good way to let other mates know that there's some b-bad news floating around too near our babies.

We like swimming, good fun that, specially out at sea, when the w-waves g-get all cross and bumpity, up and down we go. Sometimes you can't see us when we bob about in big w-waves. See, we have a lot of nice smelly oil on our feathers. Well you know that oil floats on water don't you? Yes, useful that, having oil on our feathers - keeps us floating just f-fine!

Baby-feeding time is not one of the nicest things to watch - we get kind of v-v-vomity sometimes. See we flitter off to get food, and swallow it, then we go back to the n-nest, and the little ones peck at our bills over and over again. It's enough to make you s-sick... well it does actually... make us sick I mean. We just heave up the food in our gullets and spill it right down their d-darling little throats - eeee. I 'ope this isn't making you feel all funny.

S-sorry about that.

Hard to say what I like doing the most. F-flying I guess and swimming second. Got such a nice pair of feet for swimming, nice little w-webs between my toes, great for wading and p-paddling.

It's right n-nice talking to you. I like talking, well, l-laughing I guess. Real fond of jokes, I am, I said 'jokes' not ch-chokes! Ooo, what a funny lad I am. Hey, like to hear a seagull joke? Why do seagulls fly? 'Cos you can't see gulls if they d-don't! Ooooo... *kree... kreearrrr kreearrrr*! What a joke - funny lad me. See you later, nice to meet such *gull*-ible hoomans. Look out for us, gull up on the horizon! Gull be back later oooooo... *kreeearrrr har har*... what a joke... hey, I managed to say that without s-s-stuttering! Well, gull most!

Katie the Kingfisher

## Katie the Kingfisher

*Whizzzzzzzzzzzzzzzzzzzzzzzzzz*! Bet you missed me that time. I'll fly past you again, ready?
*Zzzzzzzzzzzoooooooooooooommmmmmm*!
Pretty neat eh? I don't hang about much. Silly me, I don't hang about at all. No time, too busy, too much to do, too many places to go, up and down the river, flashing blue, white and gold, whoooopeeeeeee!

Oh all right, making your neck get tired, eh? Like watching tennis, hmmmm? I'll stop for a tick, but only for a little while, got too much to do, much too much to stay chatting like this. To be honest, I wouldn't normally stop at all, like to keep busy, but if you'll just hold out a nice stick for me, jutting out over the river, I'll stay a while. That's right, stretch it out right over the water, right there, where the water is shallow and I can get a good view of the bottom. I like that, all those little fish darting about like traffic in a busy street... hmmmmmm... nice view. Thanks!

I get a lot of comments about my colours, well, not surprisingly really, such bright colours. Not too many birds are as *blue* as I am, and you've got to admit that my flash of orange and white is quite fetching, yes? I reckon sitting about in a coat as blue as mine would get *you* noticed too! Mind you, I look at my best (though I say so myself), with great beams of sunlight on my feathers. On dull days, my blue isn't half so bright as today.

I'm sorry to say that I also get some complaints from you hoomans about being a bit on the shy side. Well, what can I say? I don't really have time to hang about and show off you know, and anyway, there aren't that many of us about, sad to say. You see, we kingfishers have very special needs when it comes to culinary things. Oh what a lovely big word! I wish I could sing words like that, but I can't. I'm afraid all my voice can do is whistle. That's a bit sad, I guess, considering how pretty I am.

Still, when you come to think about it, my long high whistle is very clever, I mean, it's the same kind of long shape of sound as the shape I make when I fly - *skreeeeeeeeeee*! - a nice long straight high sound, shrill and clear. Where was I? Oh yes, our special needs. Well, we like to eat little fish... and shrimps and frogs mainly, very yummy. That's why we like fast shallow water, especially *clear* shallow water. So nice to be able to see the little fishes swimming right under our perches.

Best place to see me - on a favourite perch, sticking out over the running water of a nice stream or river. Herbie heron spends a lot of time standing in the water, and I spend a lot of time sitting on my perch, my lovely head tilted downwards. Still, quite still, only moving my head from side to side. Sitting like I'm made of ice, not moving, mustn't move, that would frighten the fish. They are even more nervous than me and just as quick to startle and rush away! Once I spy a fish that's just my size, well, anything from about the size of your pen top to a whole pen, I get very excited and stiff, ready to drop into the water like a little blue dart. Then, if I'm really quick, I mean like a lightning flash, I can fall into the water with my wings tight by my side, and either snatch the fish in my bill, or even spear it. Oh, I know that sounds cruel, but a kingfisher's got to eat, and I don't play with the fish or anything bad like that. I then fly up to my perch with the fish in my slender bill and once I get the head facing me, I can gulp it down in a second! Oh you clever things, how did you know about me me needing to swallow the fish head first? Oh, of course, you've been talking to Herbie, and he must have told you about that!

Now perhaps you can see why I'm so shy. The fish are

shy, and so am I. They don't like big noises made by you hoomans when you stomp along the river bank, even the clodd-clop of a passing sheep will frighten them, so I keep to those nice quiet places where there's nothing but the babbling and bubbling of the water to listen to.

In the spring, I use my strong beak and my powerful feet to do something so clever. I dig a big tunnel in a river bank, or a tall bit of bank by the side of a lake. I don't like noise there either, so I choose a nice bit of soft sandy bank, hidden by lots of big fronds of grass or overhanging branches. Then my husband and I start to dig away at the soil, and make a long tunnel right into the damp soft darkness beyond the entrance.

Oh, you wouldn't, would you? I mean, you wouldn't be so silly as to try to put your arm in my nest hole, to see if I was there? Phew, what a relief. I knew I could trust you. Anyway, you wouldn't be able to get your hooman arm in because it's only a little slim tunnel really, just fat enough for me to squeeze along. At the end of the tunnel, I make a nice little room, snug and cozy, and lay my luscious creamy white round eggs in it. Not too many - only three or four - not enough time to feed more than a few babies at once. I'll bet you wonder if we ever have a wash? Well, of course we do! Nothing nicer than having a bath to wash all the dirt from our feathers, and to try to get rid of all those little creepy things that sometimes try to set up house in our plumage, what a cheek!

My garden bird cousins love you hoomans if you put some water in your garden for them to bathe in, well, even to have a drink from too! No, sorry, I can't accept your kind invitation to visit your little bird bath in your garden, not my scene at all. Well, not usually.

Oh, I forgot to mention that I live on the same river as Herbie, though if you are lucky, you could see one of us kingfishers on just about any stream, river or canal. But you'd have to have a quick eye, and *please*, be very quiet and still. I like that! The other day, I overheard those hoomans talking who have a nice house on the River Dart, right where Herbie fishes sometimes. He did the most awful thing. Do you know what? He ate their goldfish... yes... honestly... he ate them all... and I got the blame for it too... well! I mean, silly hoomans, I'm far too shy to be so silly as to fly right up to the house and steal goldfish.

Oops! What am I saying? Got to be honest, we birds never lie. If you *do* happen to have a big pond at the bottom of your garden, and it's nice and quiet and not too near the house, I *might* just get tempted. Sorry about that! See, we birds don't have such a thing as private property. We eat fish, and wherever fish are, they are just waiting to be snaffled up. There's no point in denying it.

Winter is so hard, isn't it? Ah yes, I know you hoomans *love* snow and frosts, but we don't. The water gets all stiff and hard and crinkly, and we can't get into the water to eat our breakfasts and suppers. A bad winter can see a lot of us starving and I'm afraid lots of my brothers and sisters end up in bird heaven if things go on being frozen for too long.

Of course, I'm so lucky, I found out that salty water doesn't freeze as easily as fresh water, so if the streams and rivers get all hard with frost, I fly right down the river towards the sea and get my food there. What a bit of luck, but it's very hard for those poor things who live too far away from the sea.

Well, I really must flash away, my tummy is grumbling again. Please do accept my apologies for not staying longer, but I'm a flashy kind of bird, in more ways than one, so must get on. Bye!

*ZZzzzzzzzzzzzzzzzzzzzzzip!*

*Part Two*
Garden Birds

Wally the Wren

## Wally the Wren

Hello? Hello... can you see me? No? Oh dear, am I too far away for you? Hang on a minute and I'll flutter right up to you. I'll be there in a tick!

...There, is that better? Of course it is. How daft of me not to realise that you couldn't see me over there. I'm such a little bird aren't I? You could put a couple of us wrens inside your tea cup and we'd still have room to shuffle about without getting our wings bent! You know, there *are* advantages to being very small. We can get to places that very big birds can't, which is a jolly good thing really. I can think of a *lot* of birds that I would not like to share a secret little hiding place with.

Shy? Me? Well, not really. Just small and darting that's all, and being so small you'd probably never believe that we can fly at all! Trouble is that we like to potter about on the ground a lot, so you don't see us in the air that much, not much point really.

Why? Oh you *do* ask a lot of questions! Well, why not imagine yourself lying on your tummy on the floor in some long grass, perhaps you've done that already? If you do that - and keep a sharp eye on the ground - oh my, oh my, what a busy little world you'd see.

Where I live, in a lovely big garden close to a little brushy bit of wood, you can't possibly imagine how many little creepy things there are, busying themselves in little twiggy and grass-stemmed streets and low-ways! In fact, you'd better be careful when you lie down in that long grass, because the chances are that you'll be lying right on top of at least a hundred little crawlies. There now, bet you didn't realise that? There are flies, beetles, bees, ants, aphids, thrips, wasps, cockroaches, earwigs, and... well... I could go on all day about them. All very yummy, I can assure you!

I know I'm only a tiny bird, and that's perhaps why you'd be surprised to know that there are heaps and heaps of us all over the place. It's just that we like to live in very nice bushy and shrubby kinds of haunts, where there is a lot of shadow and snuggly shade. Do you know, almost every garden in Britain could well have a pair of us bobbing in the undergrowth, or trickling in little hops and rushes across your lawns and rockeries?

Unlike those wapping great big water birds you've been talking to, we are so small that I guess you'd have a really hard time seeing our wings beat. You see, believe it or not, there are dragonflies with bodies longer than ours! Where I live, there is an enormous family of nut-brown butterflies that are almost as big as us wrens and you can *see* their wings beat much easier than you could mine.

My nice freckled and speckled dark brown feathers are great to keep me hidden from view. Much better that way. Sometimes, those very scary sparrowhawks come zooming overhead, just waiting to pounce on a poor little wren like me - oooo, makes me want to trill and tremble just thinking about it! But even with their sharp eyes, they'd have a hard time seeing me tucked away in the shadows, looking like a dead leaf or a little speck of darkness at the foot of a big fat hedge.

Ah well, everyone has their own taste. I guess even sparrowhawks have to eat. I just wish they'd pick on birds their own size. When you are tiny, a lot of things look at you in a funny kind of way, kinda thoughtful like, wondering how a small wren would taste for breakfast! Yeeow! I can't pretend to be a goody-goody in every way though. We cock wrens (that's the daddy ones, folks!) are pretty tough little critters! Woe betide any hedge sparrow or robin that gets a little too close, especially at nesting time!

That's the problem with being a garden bird. Everyone wants to sneak up and get the best spots to nest, or steal the biggest grubs from right under my beak. And don't think that I'm happy to share with other cock wrens either! *No way*! I'll see off any other wren who isn't married to me... *fast*! That's why I shout so much. Oh boy, you'd never believe that such a little bird could make such a noise. You'd think we had ghetto blasters in our chests if you got your ear close to us when we sing!

And, oh bird! What a song. Would you like me to sing you how I tell another bird that I'm in command of my own place? You would, well, here goes. I'm going to fly over there so that I don't make your head ache. Okay? Right, ready? Here goes... Tzzcht... kchooo... tzitt... shuee... shuee... rkstchee... tsu-chuar... tzee... zuit... zuit... zuit... zuit... zuit... zuit...! Did you get that? Hang on, I'll flitter back over to you.

Right, pretty good, eh? Know what I said? No? Why not? Oh, I forgot, you don't speak Birdish. That's why that nice Edward Cowie hooman came along to help translate Birdish into hooman. Well, what I said was: 'Hey! Hey! You there... yes, you lot... watch out! I'm a wren and this is my patch, so clear off... got it? Hey! yesyesyesyesyesyes!' Some birds don't seem to talk much. Herbie the heron just seems to stick to *wwaaaaaaaaaaaaaaaaatccht*. Well, it's all right for him, he's big enough for everyone to see that he's a big tough bird.

Oh, I can say lots of things. I can yell 'lookout - danger!' or (better say this quietly), 'mmmm, what a fine fellow I am, so handsome, so trim, so sexy, such a lot of fun, come on girls, what about a date?' I said that quietly because I didn't want to sound too boastful, and anyway, I don't sing those kind of messages in the autumn. Not much point, it's not a good time of year to make a nest, I mean, we'd have so much less to feed the little ones on, sometimes there is hardly enough to feed just me!

So, in the winter, most of us songbirds don't say a lot. I guess that's pretty boring for you hoomans. I know how much you like to hear us chattering away in the spring, but I bet you would be surprised if you could translate some of the things we say when we are dating ladies. Hardly polite to be honest!

Now me and my lady wife don't usually like the company of other wrens, but sometimes, to be honest, getting together in big huddles is a real life-saver. If you are big enough, a hard and bitter breath from old Jack Frost doesn't hurt you that much. But we little birds really suffer terribly from the cold. Last winter, we had some frosts that went on for days and days; brittle, sharp white icing-cake frosts, freezing everything to a standstill. My wife and I simply couldn't get warm snuggled up together. So we heard news that some other wrens had found a nice empty postbox at the edge of a hooman's garden, and that it wasn't being used. So we all slipped through the little slit at the top and well, just stacked up on top of each other like a pile of little brown fluffy bricks, if you follow my meaning. Mmmmmmmmm... such a nice warm thing to do. 'Many wrens make warm dens'. That's what Gaia taught us, bless her!

So we just stay there, all dozy and cosy, until it gets warm enough to leave, and get back to our own patches. By the way, that's a secret, so don't go sharing that around too much, okay?

No, I don't reckon that I am much of a big-head... well, with a head the size of a ten-pence piece, I couldn't be, now could I? I couldn't help overhearing snooty Serena telling you about her wonderful nest-building skills, well, they almost all did, didn't they? I reckon we wrens ought to get a special award for being the best nest builders! We collect fine pieces of moss, blades of grass, fluffy little feathers, fronds of horse hair and even strands of sheep wool, and weave them into a wondrous ball. We leave the inside hollow so that we can get inside, and make a little hole to dart in and out of.

The softest fur of hairs and feathers are made into a nice cup of silky bedding inside. Ask your mum or dad to cup their hands together, as though they were holding a tennis ball in their hands. See that? Well, that's about the size of the nests we wrens build. Now stick one of your fingers through a gap in their fingers, and you'll get a really good idea of what it feels like to dive into a wren's nest. If you get them to put a little bit of silk in one of the palms, and cup it with the other hand, that's even more what it's like inside.

The outside is hard to see, because we make sure we nest in very secret places, much better that way, keeps our young ones safe from prying eyes, and mouths! Last year my missus and me found a great place to build a nest. Some silly hooman had left a pile of nice red flowerpots inside their garden shed, and what's more they left the window a little bit open too! Well, we just couldn't help ourselves! So we built the nest inside one of the tipped-over pots. We raised eight babies last year. Pretty neat, eh?

Where are the babies now? Search me, dears! I sent them packing once they could fend for themselves and fly. Oh, come on, you can't expect us grown-ups to feed you for ever, now can you? and no, there is *not* enough nosh in the garden for all that mob to loaf around in. So, come the end of spring, it's on your wings little dears! Flit off! Or else!

Doesn't sound very nice put that way, does it? But Gaia

knows best, and anyway, they will be able to find their own place quick enough. Hey, darlings! You can help there. Make sure that you get your hooman mums and dads to leave some little places of shrubby, woody shade in your garden, a nice big fat hedge will do and we'll be there... promise.

Well, that wasn't too bad. I think I did okay there, those hoomans seemed quite nice really. Now then, let's see if I can find some little grubs to eat... what? What? Oh... I forgot... you're still there, and I didn't say cheerio...

Thanks for listening! See ya...

Flllllllllllit!

Rebecca the Robin

## Rebecca the Robin

Buzz off! Hey... clear off! I said bug off!

Oops, sorry! I wasn't talking to you. That was for Wally wren - what's he doing hanging around here anyway? Little busybody. What a cheek. I can see you, Wally, buzz off. It's my turn, and hey, leave that goat moth alone, that's mine! Hey, stop that, oh, what a cheek, he ate that moth - that was mine! Ah well, plenty more where that came from.

Well, here I am, Rebecca robin at your service. No good trying to decide whether I'm Rebecca or Robert, we look exactly the same, whether we are mums or dads, so you'll just have to take my word for it, so there. Anyway, Robert's the one who does most of the singing round here, maybe that will help? Oh, Gaia, now there's Titania the blue tit hanging around here. What's her game then?

Buzz off Titania! Yes, you wait your turn. Well, at least she won't pinch all the flies in the garden, thank Gaia, she prefers seeds! Just as well, I'd be over there and give her a quick slosh in the face if she came and stole my garden food! Oh, it's so distracting, all these birds about, waiting to talk to you, and those thrushes and blackbirds eat heaps of our food. A bit too big to rough up though, best I can do is just flit about and shout, but it makes no difference. Size wins usually!

I'm so glad to meet you. I've been wanting to thank you hoomans for all that publicity you give us robins! It's so nice of you to put us on your Christmas cards sometimes, even if you *do* have a silly habit of painting us in the snow. Can't think why you do that, surely you don't think we actually *like* snow do you? Anyway, thanks all the same. Nice to see my picture being spread around.

Oi! You there... (no not *you* hoomans!) Oi! Flap off...

that's my piece of garden... oh yes... want a peck in the wing then? Like to see my leg in your eye? Oh right! We'll see about that... just wait until I get through talking here... I'll soon show you that I mean business! Good Gaia, where's Robert? *He* should be dealing with all these scroungers.

Whoops, I had better watch my tongue, you might just think that we robins are on the tough side. Little brown and red toughos, or something like that. Honestly, I'm a sweet little thing really... well... some of the time. Except when one of those blinking hedge sparrows or blue tits gets into my patch... **THEN I REALLY SEE RED, IF YOU KNOW WHAT I MEAN... AND I MEANT IT... YOU LOT THERE! PACK THAT UP! CLEAR OFF OR I'LL BASH YOU UP, GOT IT?**

Oh dear, me and my temper! Just can't help myself. Those greedy birds. You'd think they'd know about dangerous *red*, now wouldn't you? Ooo my! I'm all fluffed up to twice my size; just furious, really cross now.

Now, where was I? Ah... hmmmm... I'll just take a few nice slow breaths and calm down... I'm almost out of breath with temper... that's better. Talking of thank yous... thanks also for the lovely gardens you hoomans make - and a really *big* thank you for the nosh in the winter. I don't know how some of us would manage if you didn't put that food out for us on your bird tables. Only *please* stop calling them *titbits*, okay? It makes me go red just thinking about that silly name. Titbits? Call them Robinbits. that's okay. But NOT titbits.

Now, we robins are very jealous birds. Not too happy

with sharing things, and if that naughty Wally wren conned you into thinking that *he's* a paragon of virtue, forget it. A right little cruising bruiser *he* can be as well. We robins and wrens often get into a scrap over space. I'm always giving him a *ticking off,* and I mean just that. When I'm cross, I *tick* like a clock that's going to bust a spring, especially in spring (oooo - a robin-joke!) and I also do a lot of ticking in the autumn too, just to make sure that no other robins or garden birds are going to be silly enough to think of moving in. Not a good idea at all, I give 'em heaps of bother.

I know you hoomans have been hearing some *big* words lately. What a clever owl our Ambassador is! Well, here's one for you, a nice big word of our own: *territorial.* That's right, *terri-tor-rial*! that's a big word that means that we guard our nesting and feeding places for ourselves, that's why we shout such a lot and get into fights.

Mind you, this getting cross has its nice side, we robins are one of the few birds that sing nice songs in the winter as well. Not so long as in the spring, but a lot longer than most other songbirds during the cold months.

My song is like a little tinkling bell, making a shape like sugar pouring down from a thin spout. Can you imagine that? It makes me come over all gentle and soft, thinking about how nice my song is. So why do we sing so much? Hmmmmm... well that's easy really. Like you hoomans, we birds rely a lot on seeing and hearing. Now, in the case of us robins, well you can't miss that blushing red breast now, can you, but a lot of us can't see who's in the trees around us. So we sing loudly, just to let others know where we are.

I heard Wally telling you about his fancy nest. I have to admit that wrens *do* make a real splash with their little homes, but then, so do we robins! I build a beautiful neat little cup of leaves, grasses, feathers and hairs too, but honestly, I just can't be bothered to put a roof on mine! I can't see the point myself. I mean, I always choose a nice little nook or cranny, with plenty of shelter over the top to keep the rain out.

What a relief it was to us birds that you hoomans stopped pinching our eggs! What a silly idea, stealing our babies from us, and sticking the eggs in drawers to go all mouldy and break! What a waste of life, I mean, *we* have mums and dads too you know and *please*, don't disturb us when we are nesting! I hate to have little hands pawing all over my nest, and you'd be surprised how many nosy animals there are, just waiting for you hoomans to show them where we have our babies. So don't do it, there's nice dears!

By the way, do you hoomans fly away on holiday much? Oops - of course you don't fly... well... but *do* you go over the sea at all? You do? Well, don't be surprised to find lots of us robins over there as well. In fact most birds that are going to talk to you today live in France, Germany, Spain and all that. I know that there are other kinds of robins all over the world, but I'm afraid I'm not clever enough to work out why they look different from me. It's one of Gaia's secrets.

Oh Gaia! There's a great big thrush sitting just over there... ooo dear... a bit on the big side for my liking! More than twice my size, so I'd better make myself scarce and go and see off those other small birds over there who just don't seem to get the message that this is my patch... and that I don't like them fooling around in my garden... trying to steal all those lovely flies.

...so bug off!

## Yes... you!
# FLIT OFF!

Thomas the Song Thrush

## Thomas the Song Thrush

Hello there! Hello there! How are you doing? How are you doing? Okay? Okay? Nice to meet you. Nice to meet you. What a nice day. What a nice day. Lovely to be here. Lovely to be here. Yes! Yes! I just love singing. I just love singing. Tops of trees. Tops of trees. Best place to sing. Best place to sing. Yippee! Yippee! Oh what fun. Oh what fun. Yes! Yes!

Gaia me, I'm quite out of breath. If I hadn't got a breast covered in freckled spots already, I'd come out in them all over! I'm so excited to be talking to you, I'm so excited to be talking to you, I'm so excited to be talking to you, oops, just can't help repeating myself. I love things that rhyme, you see, just *love* to sing things that repeat, over and over again, over and over again!

Do you have any of my brothers and sisters near you? Any of us ever visit your garden? You know, I have a sad tale to tell. We thrushes were once very easy to see, just about everywhere, especially where we could find tasty worms, snails and slugs to eat! But something terrible has happened, we seem to be slowly vanishing - Help! Help!

I've asked our wise Ambassador owl what the problem is, but he doesn't know either. Surely you hoomans can help us? My great-great-great-great-great grandparents used to sing songs about fields with lovely *big* hedges, all around them. But you silly hoomans have been digging them up all over the place, and I reckon this is a *real* shame. How would you like it if great big bulldozers came and dug up all your grocery stores, eh?

And another really sad thing, you know, we thrushes have a very good sense of taste, but we never realised that you hoomans were putting those horrid sprays all over your crops! Full of nasty things that either kill us grown-ups or worse, stop our eggs from having healthy babies in them.

Now surely, now surely, that's a very silly thing, that's a very silly thing? Don't you *want* us to sing in your gardens anymore? Don't you want to see us sitting in the very tops of stately shrubs and trees, singing our little hearts out? *Promise* that you'll care for us... *please*?

You know, we eat heaps of things that eat your garden flowers and crops. Me? Me? Give me some nice fat snails and I'm happy, and I'm happy, I'm happy, happy! I snatch them from under big leaves and stones, I snaffle them from inside cracks in walls and under damp logs, and then I take them to my favourite piece of stone or hard tree trunk, and I bash and bash and bash, until the shell breaks, then I can gobble up the delicious insides of them. Might sound yucky to you, but birdie heaven to us!

And, oh Gaia! I love to hop delicately on your nice smooth lawns and feel the vibrations through my toes. Yes, honestly, yes, honestly, I can even feel a worm moving down there. Then, when one gets too close to the surface, I snap my beak shut, and slowly draw it out of the ground, like sucking up spaghetti! Oh yum, oh yum, give me a worm, give me a worm!

We thrushes are so famous that some of your hooman poets have written such nice words about us. Mind you, I'm not too sure I like the poem that says that we are 'terrible'. What? What? Us? Us? How can that be? Maybe we are terrible to a snail, but surely not to you hoomans? Nothing more thrilling than a trilling willing thrush! Hmmmm, that was nice to say. Can you say it? Go on, try... 'A thrilling trilling willing thrush.' Well done! Clever you.

In the winter, I get awfully quiet. You won't hear me saying much at all. It's a nice time of year though, because some of our thrushy cousins come for a winter visit, oh... from a long way to the east and north where the snows are deep and there's no food.  Our cousins, the redwings and fieldfares, look a lot like us, honestly, except that they stay in big parties and party on in the open fields and meadows.  Not like us.

We do have two kinds of cousins who stay here all year round like us though.  One is the mistle thrush.  They look a *lot* like us, but a little bigger, and perhaps a teeny bit less spotty!  And hey, guess what?  Blackbirds are our cousins too but my good friend Brenda blackbird will tell you about that in a while.  She's sitting on top of the  hedge just over there.  I'll just wave to her, I'll just wave to her.  Oh how nice, oh, how nice, she waved back!

Now I know you've realised that I like to repeat things, to repeat things, repeat things.  Sometimes I sit on top of a high branch and just sing for ages, sing for ages... sing for ages!  In fact the older I get, the more things I seem to be able to sing.  Well to be honest, I really *have* to learn to sing more!  Why?  Well, it has to do with the dating scene!  You see, lady thrushes like to date the best singers.  You know, the ones with the best things to sing.

Hmmmm... yes, I realise that you young hoomans probably haven't started dating yet, but I'm sure, I'm sure you'll understand.  When you *do* decide to take one of your nice hooman chicks out on a date... well... I mean... you *do* chat them up, I'm sure, I'm sure.  Surely, there's a *good* way to chat someone up, and a not-so-good way?  It's no good me just going up to a nice sexy lady thrush and just saying 'hey-hey, what about a date?  What about a date?' It just doesn't seem to work!  I mean, suppose you find spots sexy... well I do anyway!

It's no use at all just sitting on top of a twig and looking lovingly across at some swell thrush chick and singing, 'hey spotty!' or, 'wow! wow! Nice spots!' they just don't seem to get turned on by little dull messages like that. So I have to try all the best bits of fancy talk that I can. Now I'm three years old, and I've had lots of time to get *really* good at the dating game. This year, I saw a great-looking lady thrush sitting in the branches of a beech tree on my patch - wow... was she a good-looker, good-looker!

So I found my best perch, right in the very highest bit of a tall ash tree, and found myself singing this; 'oh what a lovely day, oh what a lovely day... golden sunshine, golden sunshine... lights up your feathers... I can see your spots, I can see your spots... so nice, so nice... ravishing, ravishing... got me all exited, got me all excited, sophisticated, sophisticated... suave, suave... you turn me on, turn me on, turn me on... how lovely, how lovely you look, how lovely you must be... must be, must be.'

Well, you've got to admit, that's a lot better isn't it? It worked a treat, it worked a treat. Before I knew it, we were busy nest building in a wonderful thick piece of bramble patch. We found a good bit that we could wedge twigs and grass into, and slowly built up a nice deep cup, about the same size as the bowl you eat your Corn Flakes in. Then, when we had finished that bit, we buzzed off down to find some nice wet mud, and lined the inside of the nest with that. It makes the nest very tough and strong.

When the mud got really nice and dry, my missus laid some lovely sky-blue eggs in it, lovely light blue, lovely light blue... with lots of little black spots on them - ooo - I love spots! I love spots. We had five eggs this year, and they all hatched. Got to confess this, the first time I saw our babies hatch a year ago, I nearly threw up! Oh Gaia, you've never seen such ugly critters! Pink little gremlins with scarcely a feather in sight, only a few little wispy hairs, and, surprise, surprise, they couldn't even open their eyes.

There I was, just wanting to look into their darling eyes and say, 'hi chicks... hi chicks, I'm your dad... I'm your dad... see? See?' And they just flopped about with their eyes shut and seemed to be able to say only two words over and over again - 'feed me, feed me'. Not so much as a 'thank you', or a dinner order, or what they wanted for breakfast. Just boring old 'feed me!' Well, I mean to say! I mean to say! What a shock. Thank goodness they grew up pretty fast, and within a few days, they *could* see what a handsome dad they had.

The rest of that spring was a bit of a blur to me, can't remember ever being so tired: up at the crack of dawn, up to my high singing posts, yelling a lot of messages about being in love, and telling those other daddy thrushes to buzz off from *my* patch, and then start the hunt for food for the babies, then more singing, then more food for babies, more singing, more food for babies, more singing, time for a quick bite for me, more singing, more feeding... Oh Gaia!

If a thrush could blush, if a thrush could blush, I would right now. Drove me nuts, that first spring as dad! The great day came though, when the babies got on the edge of the nest and flew for the first time. 'Whoopee', I thought 'that's them gone!' Well, you won't believe this, but the little beggars just kept on chasing my wife around and yelling for food! What a cheek, well, I mean! Yes, we kept on feeding them, but less at a time. They soon got the message. I sat at the top of a pine tree, and started some new songs, I can tell you. 'Hoy, you lot... feed yourselves, feed yourselves... over there, over there... that's right, that's right... nice fat snails... help yourself, help yourself'. Worked really well that. They soon got the message.

Now I don't really have any gripes about you hoomans except the bit about leaving us some nice hedges, and stopping all that nasty poison from getting into us. But there is just *one* more little thing I really must share with you, must share with you. You hoomans seem to have a real thing about glass, can't see why, but you do. I mean you have all those big bits of glass in those square holes in your nests - *windows* I believe you call them?

Sometimes you make them so clean that we thrushes can't see that they are solid and hard. In fact from our side, they often seem like great big pieces of sky and trees, so I'm afraid that once in a while one of us thrushes or some other garden bird will fly right into them, and get hurt. Some even hit them so hard that they end up in birdy heaven. Now I know many of you hoomans are actually very kind, very kind and when we do bash into a window, you rush out to see if we are okay. Well, take a bit of advice - don't bother, don't bother!

Far better to just leave us to recover on our own. You hoomans are so big and scary close up. You'd only make things worse if you came up close, and worse still if you picked us up and moved us. Most of us just sit there and look dazed and dopey. Well you would be dopey if you crashed into a window at twenty miles an hour! But just take a grip on yourselves, and stay where you are. Nine times out of ten, in a few minutes, we'll get our breath back, and fly off just fine. Please pass that on, there's good hoomans!

Next spring I'll be four, and the best thrushy singer in this neck of the woods and gardens. Lady thrushes don't sing much at all, so don't go getting all mixed up and thinking that they do! A few chirps and squeaks, and that's it for lady thrushes. Most daddy birds do all the singing, because we are the ones who defend the places where we eat and have babies, but hey, do just sit and listen, sit and listen, and listen to one of us song thrushes next spring, okay? Can't miss us, can't miss us. Got to dash, got to dash, just spotted a fat worm, just spotted a fat worm. See you! Bye! Bye!

Brenda the Blackbird

## Brenda the Blackbird

*!ereht iH. uoy teem ot eciN...* Oh dear, me and my dyslexia! Just can't help getting my letters all mixed up sometimes - yrros! And I'm better much not words with too. Singing lovely is but. Okay dears, I'll *really* try to get my words out straight, oooo... I did it! this is a strange thing to say, I know, but I'm not actually black at all! We lady blackbirds are soft dark brown in colour, and if you look very closely, you'll see that we have lovely speckled feathers on our breasts, and just a hint of a pale creamy white collar, like a crescent moon on our lower neck. I don't know how we got the name *black*bird, except to say that daddy blackbirds *are* as black as coal and jet. That's the *stone* jet, dears.

What's more, daddy blackbirds have bills the same colour as rose hips, as orange as an orange in fact. Oh, aren't I doing well? I haven't got a single letter or dorw mixed up yet? Whoops! I meant *word*! Sorry. Now, daddy thrushes and mummy thrushes look the same, but we blackbirds don't. Confusing, I guess, especially if you happen to be a thrush! You hoomans would get pretty mixed up, if you all looked the same now wouldn't you? Well, as our French brothers and sisters say in France, '*vive la difference*!'

Most often, you hoomans meet us blackbirds in your gardens and parks. I guess because thrushes and blackbirds are related, we eat pretty well the same things, and behave very much like each other, you know, hop and walk the same way, and even sing with very similar voices. Mind you, I *do* envy thrushes sometimes. They are so clever at getting their words out in rhymes, and repeating them over and over again so that they sound nice. Actually, I think they do that because they are forgetful!

They say the same things two or three times, because they can't remember what comes next!

Just kidding, dears! No, we blackbirds sing our words all jumbled up, hardly repeating a word at all, when we really let go. Me? Well I don't sing that much as a matter of fact. I leave that to the daddy ones. Honestly, they sing so much, we ladies can't get a warble in edgeways! Oo, it's so *hard* to keep talking to you like this. I simply *have* to talk a little blackbird for a minute, just to get my poor brain to work properly. Better is that... much like more do I... strange me seems is wonderful able to songs of in out order... because... understand better much words chaos pattern me for... phew, that's better! You know, I should really fly off right now. I mean Thomas the song thrush is so much better at talking to you than I am, makes me want to cry really. I hate repeating myself, I hate saying the same thing twice.

Trouble is, we blackbirds do so many of the same things that thrushes do, it's hard to sound as different as all that. We live in the same places as they do, you see, and *where* we live is a lot to do with *what* we do there, if you follow my meaning. Mind you, I have to confess that I'm not a snailoholic! Ugh! They're okay to eat if you are desperate, but not my scene really. I prefer worms and insects myself.

I couldn't help overhearing Thomas telling you about his tastes, and do you know, he forgot to mention that he and I also like to eat berries! Well, how could he forget that? Hawthorn berries, ivy berries, elderberries, blackberries - oh yum! And thank you *so much* for growing all those beak-watering strawberries, raspberries and currents in your garden! How nice of you. Saves such a lot of trouble searching about when you just put that great nosh in your fruit patch. And hey! do you *have* to put those nets all over them to keep us out? I mean, makes things so hard to hop about and find a little hole to creep through. Why grow blackbird yummies, if we can't just fly right down and eat them? You hoomans are so funny sometimes!

I know we *have* to tell you the truth about ourselves, so I'd better confess that we are a little more short-tempered than our thrushy cousins. Now, what did I mean by that? Well come on dears, you *know* what I mean. We get a bit scrappy and rough once in a while! Nothing nicer than a little fight in the garden. Mind you, we fight anywhere really. See, we don't *just* live in your gardens and parks. You could see one of us just about everywhere where there are nice big hedges or trees and shrubs. Anywhere where worms, bugs, beetles and berries live, in fact.

What do we fight about? Hey, don't be beaky! Whoops. I mean, don't be nosy! Oh all right then - we fight over food and space mainly, and sometimes the guys get a bit jealous and bash each other up over us ladies! You can tell when we have a scrap because we whizz and whirl about like maniacs, feathers and wings flying in all directions, leaping up and down and round and round, sometimes on the ground and sometimes even in the air. No, don't worry, no harm done. We don't normally hurt each other, just a game you know. A pity you hoomans don't settle your differences like that!

Everybirdy seems to be boasting about their nests today! I can understand that - we birds are great architects you know. I mean we make things that can stand the winds and the rain, and that protect our babies from sneaking things as well. Normally, I like to build *my* nest somewhere hard to find, you know, hidden in shady little nooks in hedges or in the dark shady bits of tree trunks and branches. Sometimes though, you hoomans make some great spots for us to nest - in your woodsheds, even on a shelf in your garage. So long as you don't have one of those blinking cats about. Now I *hate* cats!

oH-hO... whoops... I mean Oh-Ho! You've noticed that Herbie heron builds a nest where it's easy to see it? Well, big birds can make nests more in the open than we do. I mean, they are so big, and hey, they build their nests in big housing estates, so no problem! Of course, birds like the crows and those nasty buzzards build their nests solo, and you can see them, but ah, ah, ah, I mean ha, ha, ha, you couldn't *reach* them now could you?

Because we build our nests so close to the ground, we simply *have* to build them as hidden as possible. If we didn't, every ferret, weasel, hawk, rat, magpie, jay, owl, buzzard, kestrel, stoat, fox, eagle and cat would be on to us like a shot, and steal the babies from right under our beaks!

Take a look at one of my nests; a neat cup of woven grasses, twigs and leaves, lined with hairs and feathers and moss. About the same size and shape as a thrush's nest, but without that yucky mud inside. Neat, eh? You know, all we have to build with is our beaks and feet. It takes *ages* to get each little bit to fit with another bit. But somehow, we manage to slide the twigs and grasses into each other so that they lock together just like a mat or carpet. Same idea, really, knit one, purl one, knit one, purl one.

At night time, we have a kip, just like you hoomans. Now I know there's not much point in you going bird watching at night, because, well, you *won't see much*! And apart from my bird relatives that like messing about at night-time, the rest of us find a nice cuddly place, and close our eyes. One thing I'm sure of though, you hoomans, I bet we get up a lot earlier than you do!

We birds know a lot about light, and it takes the teeniest tiny bit of change of light to cause us to wake up, and start shuffling our feathers. You hoomans usually need a wet cold cloth on your faces, or a quick bash with a soft pillow before you get out of bed, but not us! As soon as the light looks a little like the sun is on its way, we are off our perches, and away to get some fastbreak... oops - I mean breakfast!

Now, I really do have a tired brain. It's been very hard to talk to you like this, so I do hope that you won't mind me getting on with my jobs for the day? Anyway, here comes Charlie, and he's just unstoppable when it comes to chatting. Bye so better going get!

Charlie the Chaffinch

# Charlie the Chaffinch

*Pink! Pink! Pink! Pink! Pink! Pink!*

Hi there!  Like my little song?  Ever noticed that I sing that colour all the time, over and over again?  *Pink! Pink!*

Of course you have!  Not surprising really, I mean, I love pink, one of my favourite colours, in fact.  A lot of my feathers are pink, hundreds of them, then there's blue, well, I like that too - I have lots of blue feathers on my head and neck.  Oh it's great being a finch!  Most of us are so colourful.

You've got to claw it to me, I am a real good-looker, that's for sure.  Not so flashy as Bill the bullfinch, who's as red as a strawberry with a head as black as coal, but oh boy!  I'm pretty all right!  and if I may be so bold, I keep a much trimmer figure than Bill, who often looks a little... how shall I put it...?  Plump!  It must be all those cherry flower buds he eats, and apple blossoms which I gather makes you hoomans real mad.  Can't blame you really!

In the bad old days, we pretty finches had a real hard time because you hoomans put us in cages.  Now I ask you, that's not nice is it?  You hoomans can be very silly you know.  Do you *really* think we sing and look better in a cage, unable to fly, unable to show you how we behave in the wild?  Thank goodness you have laws now that have put a stop to all that nonsense.  And worse still, you actually stuffed us and put us in glass cases, and I even heard a rumour that you used to wear us on your ladies' hats?  You can't be serious?  *On your HATS*?  I don't believe it, you can't have been *that* funny!  Or should I say nasty?

What did Brenda talk about?  Not much, I bet!  I can't understand a word she sings to tell the truth, except when she goes about *clicking* a lot, like a little stone being dropped into a jam jar - oo, that was clever of me - to think of that! All of us birds have special songs that we use sometimes. Very short songs, like my lovely *pink, pink!* It's our way of sending messages fast and easily. Each of the bird families has their own little message, and I believe you hoomans have funny names for some of these. I think the funniest is *sub-song*! Makes me chuckle that, sub-song? What ever do you mean?

Oh all right, I was joking. I know why you call our little short songs sub-song. *Sub* is one of your old words from the Romans who roamed about all over the place hundreds of years ago. They spoke a funny language too, which I believe you call *Latin*? Well *sub* means *under* in Latin, so I suppose you mean that our sub-song is kind of 'under' our best long songs, like it's not so full, not so good? Now that's kind of true you know. I mean, in the spring, I sing a *lovely* long song. Your nice hooman translator, Edward Cowie, helped me to write that down like this, *chit-chit-chit-chooree...tak-tak-tak-tar-ar*! You've got to say that real fast. Now, in different places, we chaffinches don't say that in quite the same way. I live in Suffolk you see, but chaffinches in Scotland say that just a little bit differently, especially the little bit at the end. Why? Hmmmmmm... well you hoomans have something called *surnames* don't you? Right! Well, if you *hear* the name, MacGregor, you'd expect that person to come from where? Scotland. Clever you! If a person was called Reese, I know, that's a hard one. Try Owen, or Hughes? Got it? Wales, that's right, and if you hear the sound *Grunwald*, where might that person come from? Germany. Right!

Well, we chaffinches have special local messages that help the ladies to know who they are dating. It's not usual for a lady chaffinch who lives in Suffolk to date with a guy from Ireland! Well, they *couldn't* anyway, too far away! But because we live in different places, we sing with a slightly different pattern of song. Neat, eh? Bet you didn't know that.

Oh, I do go on a bit, don't I? Well, a bit more about our song talks. In the autumn, things get a little bit on the rough side, weather wise. There's not so much nosh as in the spring and summer, so there's not so much to talk about, and the lady chaffinches go all kind of remote and claw-offish. They don't seem to be interested in making a nest at all, and the other guys don't bother to get all touchy and cross about space.

So, we get a bit of rest from all that stuff, and have a nice quiet time. I sing-talk a little, but nothing like the lush songs I use in the spring. Most birds are like that, so all you'll hear in the winter is little bits of talk, every now and then, and it's really hard to tell who's singing!

Hey, anyone talked to you about beaks? Oh, Herbie did? Well, you can't miss *his* beak, now can you. He'd need a very long handkerchief to blow his nose with! And what about Mavis mallard's beak? Well, bill actually. I mean she uses it like a spoon or fork in the water, just right for shovelling and dabbling. Now we finches have beaks like nutcrackers! Oh ho, what am I saying? They *are* nutcrackers! Well, seed crackers anyway. Yep, we just *love* seeds. We eat seeds from almost any plant, pulling them off with our beaks, then cracking them open and eating the scrumptious soft bits inside. I know you hoomans eat lots of seeds at Christmas, like walnuts and hazel nuts. Hey, better not let the squirrels know about that! And I know you use those funny bits of metal tong things to crack the hard cases open with.

Well, I'm going to make a finch-joke here. *Snap!* Pink-pink-pink-pink! Yes, snap! Our beaks are big and heavy, like nutcrackers. We might be little enough to sit inside your teacup, but oh bird, have we got strong beaks! I don't turn down the odd insect mind you, and I just *love* getting some juicy things from your bird tables! Thanks very much.

We get together in quite big gangs in the winter. Last year, there were more than twenty of us hanging around and chewing on beech nuts and grass seeds, yep, guys and girls, makes no difference. Of course, we guys are the really colourful ones. Sorry about that ladies! My lady wife last year was such a lush chick. Lovely nutty grey feathers, and the most sexy little white bits on her wing. A great turn-on when she flew about, flapping those silky white feathers on her shoulders!

Now when it comes to flying, well, we're pretty good at it actually. I've even learned how to do the loop the loops like our flycatcher cousins, you know, when chasing a nice fly or something? Mind you, I'm afraid I'm not too good at getting peanuts from your feeders. I can't get the *hang* of it. Oh, pink! pink!

Come the spring and its whoopee time! I get my voice going at its most tinkly best, even before the leaves come on the trees, and chortle away to my little heart's content. That's the time to put on my brightest colours, oh yes, the brightest I can make them. I lift my little slate-grey crest, bob about, flap my wings, and make such a lovely fuss of all those chaff chicks that hang around.

Our nest isn't that much bigger than one of your hooman's egg cups, which of course is what my nest is - an egg-cup! *Tee-hee!* The missus and me make it together, taking a lot of time to find a nice little nook in a tree branch most often. Bend your arm and make an 'L' shape; done that? Well, get something like a little ball, or an apple and try to hold it in the little wedge you've made.

Done that?  Great!  That's why we like to find a little 'L' in a tree to wedge the nest in.

I'm not good at counting, but most times out of most times we nest higher than you could reach from the ground.  Now don't go blaming *me*, it's not my fault.  Too many other creatures down there that can climb and nosh on our chicks.  So there!  Lovely soft lining of hairs and feathers inside the nest, to keep the little finchy babies' bottoms warm!  Oh bird, can they eat!  We're just exhausted by the end of each day, feeding at least as many babies as you have fingers on one hand, however many that is.

Now, I don't know what you hoomans do about keeping clean, I mean, I haven't seen many of you just getting into water and splashing your feathers to get clean!  The only time I've seen that is when I once went to a big river, and saw lots of hooman chicks gallumping about in the water.  Is that when you wash?

Well, I can't swim like Mavis can, or even Herbie for that matter.  Don't seem to float very well to be honest!  So when I wash, I choose some nice little bit of water that I can stand in and flutter and flip so that the water gives me a nice cold shower.  See?  We birds are *very* clean really.  Hey, do put a little bit of water by your bird table.  I promise I'll use it, honestly!

We keep the babies clean too and I know you might find this a little yucky... but... well... well... I mean... to be honest... my kids last year were a right little bunch of... well... to put it this way... well... poopers!  Couldn't think of any other way to put that.  We grown-ups can just do that from a nice twig or branch, but the very little ones can't even get their little pink bottoms over the side of the nest.

So the little darlings wait until we are feeding them, lift up their little bottoms, and well... poop!  Got to be real quick to catch it, but we always do, and fly off with it in our beaks and drop it somewhere nice and far from the nest. See, we birds are very clean. Germs you see, lots of nasty crawlies that would get into the nest and hurt the little darlings if we didn't keep the place clean. *Hiss-joani-ic*... I call it... no! *High-beam-fit*... no... oh, I know the word I want... *hygienic*... yes, that's it... hygienic.

Now I don't think that you hoomans actually lay eggs? Why ever not? Seems a load of finch sense to me! Anyway, we lay eggs (well, not me actually, I'm a fella!) and they are all spotted and pretty. You could put three of our eggs on your teaspoon, but you'd better not! Pinching eggs is NOT ON. Got that!

Well, I've been finchin' on, haven't I? Hmm... interesting that you hoomans come out with such funny expressions. Better get going. The sun is out, so I'd better make the most of it and grab some lunch. See ya!

Now let me see, what rhymes with *pink*? Tink? Blink? Kink? Wink? Sink? Oh Gaia! I hate those. I'll just stick to *pink*, I think!

Titania the Blue Tit

## Titania the Blue Tit

### ...zzzzzzzzzzzzzzzzzzzzzzzzzzzzzzzip!

Oh my... oh my... oh my! My turn *at last*! I've been hanging around here for ages, waiting for this, and I mean *hanging*! I tried waving upside down from that big laurel bush, I tried hanging from the big cherry tree, and I even tried hanging from that bird feeder over there, and *still* you hoomans were too busy to notice me! It's just not fair, keeping a funny girl like me waiting for so long.

All those noisy birds; croaking, hissing, screaming, bubbling, wittering, warbling. I thought they'd *never* stop yacketing on with you. I just hung upside down, thinking to myself that you hoomans would just fall over with boredom! 'They'll give up and go to bed, long before I get my chance to speak', I said to myself. Well, how wrong can a girl be? Here you still are, and here I am.

I got so excited when Ambassador owl chose me to speak, that I rushed right off to bash up a couple of greenfinches and a hedge sparrow, just in sheer joy! Rushed right up to them I did. Flapped my wings, did a great big yawn or two with my bill, flicked my tail, and clattered a whole lot of bleep words at them, I did. Scared 'em to bits actually.

See the way I reckon this is that they're just jealous. Yes, that's it - *jealous*. I mean, everybody knows that we blue tits are top of the pops! In the bird charts of you hoomans we get star billing, and so we should, so there. Oh, I know hoomans get all sloppy and goofy when they hear Thomas the song thrush sing, and get a bit gaga, at the sight of Katie kingfisher, but let's face it, we blue tits have the biggest hooman fan club of the lot.

Look, we are the funniest, cleverest, prettiest, friendliest, most splendiferous of all the birds I know. Yep, we are! Who'd have thought that such little teeny birds could be so popular? *Tszit*! Yoo-hoo! Hey there, Charlie! Look at me now. See? These hoomans just love me. Hey! Charlie? Oh well, get lost then, you're next on my bashing list!

Oh come on now. Don't get all coy and defensive on me. Don't pretend you hoomans don't like a little bit of a scrap now and then? The other night, I slept in a hazel bush, right outside one of your hooman's places and I saw what you were watching on one of those funny square flashing things in your sitting room. You just sat there, like you were frozen still or something, and watched some hooman bash up a lot of other hoomans, and he did it to music as well. So I mean, well, you *must* like watching the odd scrap, so don't say you don't.

Mind you, I really can't understand why you hoomans actually *hurt* each other - what? How silly! We don't have to do that - we just *look* and *sound* like we are actually bashing each other up, but that's all show really. Hey! Better keep that a secret, okay? Bad news if all those other garden birds thought we were faking it! I guess you think we blue tits are a bit tough? Hmmmm... depends on what you think 'tough' is! *All* birds tend to squabble, usually over nosh or nests, which is another way of saying food or sex!

Well, think about it, when do hoomans squabble? On the playground, right? Two of you want to play on the same swing, not enough room for two? Right, get cross and squabble! Your mum or dad make the best yummy mashed potatoes and you and your sister or brother want the last extra helping, so what do you do? Yes, squabble over it!

And when you get older, and you *both* fancy the same boy or girl hooman. What do you do then? Right on!

Squabble! Same as us blue tits, and though you hoomans really are kind to put food out for us in the hard winter months, well, you really are asking a lot of us when you put the food inside such little things to grab the peanuts and fat from! Everybirdy wants some, and there simply isn't room for all of us to fit at the same time. So what do we do? Squabble!

It's not always like that. We do have a lot of fun, really we do, and one of the main reasons why we are so popular is because we play a lot. I think we are the comedy acts in your garden, much more than our close cousins, the great tits. Hey, whilst I think of it, what's all this *great* tit bit? What a beak! Great? Them? Huh! Oh, sorry, you mean they're *bigger* than us blue tits... oh, I see... 'great' means bigger? Oh that's okay then. You got me a bit cross there for a flappond or two. I was about to stick my little feathers up on the top of my blue head and look all cross!

It's just that we don't like getting mixed up with our tit cousins - so many of them stick their beaks into our garden space - what a pain in my tail feathers! Last winter, we had to put up with a whole bunch of long tailed tits in the garden. What a beak! They don't even live in the garden normally, and I don't know many of 'em that would be seen dead nesting in a hooman garden, unless you were silly enough to leave a lot of brambles about, but then, you don't do that much do you?

Now, there they were, a cute family of about... well, a lot of them, flitting about like butterflies with little pale straws flying behind them... and they made a right mess of the bread and nuts that you hoomans put out for us popular blue tits! Just because they have tails that are longer than their bodies they think they own the place - what a beak. They're no bigger than me really, just all tail and that's that!

Okay, they *are* pretty with black and white bodies, and a little blush of pink on their feathers, but do they really look as good as me? Not likely! At least they have the good manners to sing-talk differently from me. I hate those coal tits and great tits who pinch so many of my bits of songs, except that they just add a bit, or repeat a bit more than we do. What a beak! And what I want to know is this, who gave great tits permission to pinch our blue colouring? Oops - Gaia, eh? Enough said, I'll keep my beak shut on that one then!

Anyway, one thing is for certain, *we* are the bluest birds in your gardens... well... so long as you don't count Jimmy the jay, in my garden, that is. I must confess, he has the most gorgeous blue flashes, like a row of medals on his wings but, oh Gaia, he's such a meany! You'd think he'd be happy eating all those great big acorns and seeds all around, but does that keep him happy? No way! He eats anything. Anything! It's disgusting, really it is.

Last year he sat and watched Henrietta hedge sparrow build such a cute nest in the lonicera at the bottom of the garden. He just sat there, looking all innocent, and even had the cheek to look busy! Well, I tried to warn Henrietta, but she just didn't get it. Well *she* didn't get it, but Jimmy jay jolly well did! Waited, he did, until poor Henrietta's chicks were nice and fat, and swooped down and ate the lot! So much for the acorns bit!

I twittered with Henrietta afterwards, when she'd moved and built a new nest down by the river bank, and offered to show her how to fix Jimmy jay *and* Maggie the magpie (she's just as bad as those beaky jays). I told her that we blue tits find a nice little hole in a tree, just wide enough to squeeze our little fluffy bodies through, and that we bash our beaks inside the hole to make it wider and deeper, then line the bottom with soft grass and feathers and hairs.

Hard though he might try, there just isn't any way that Jimmy can get in *there*! But silly Henrietta, she just did the same thing again. No idea if she raised any chicks that year, I was too busy to find out. I married Terry blue tit last year, and what a dish he was! Nobody danced better than him, and oh bird, what a voice. We tried a new nest place that year, and rented a nice little box with a hole in it that one of you hoomans put there. No idea why you'd do such a strange thing. I mean, that little box was just the right height off the ground, and we didn't even have to get fat beaks knocking the hole into shape! Odd that.

I laid a heap of eggs, more than the number of claws on my two feet, and they did just fine! I sat for about sunrise, sunrise, sunrise, sunrise, sunrise, sunrise, sunrise, sunrise, sunrise, sunrise, sunrise, sunrise, sunrise, sunrise and then the eggs got all noisy and little cracks appeared, and darling little beaks came through the pearly-white shells, and out popped our chicks. Oh Gaia! Heaven!

Thank goodness we had a lot of juicy caterpillars and bugs about that year. Lots of times I got dizzy with the effort, really I did. Terry and me worked so hard that sometimes we both arrived at the same time, and one of us had to queue up whilst the other was inside the box feeding our little darlings. And even when the little ones were out of the box and flitting about, they just kept following us and begging for food. I can't remember when they finally got fed up, or rather, un-fed up, and started feeding themselves, but it was a relief, I can assure you!

Now there *is* something that I'm supposed to twitter to you about. Ambassador owl said that there used to be complaints from you hoomans about something we blue tits did. *Complain*? About US? How were we to know you didn't put those lovely big glass and foil things on your doorstep for us to drink milk from? I think our Ambassador has got that wrong. In fact, it only goes to show how smart we blue tits are, that we could use our sharp beaks to rip off the shiny caps and drink our milk for breakfast! Anyway, you naughty hoomans seem to have given that nice trick up in most places, which is real mean, I reckon.

I wouldn't want you hoomans to think that we depended on you for our living, you know. Just because we like your gardens, doesn't mean that we don't like just about every-where else to live. Mind you, you've got to claw it to us, we are real *friendly* - when we do live near you, which must be nice, surely. Nobody is going to get *me* to give up *my* nice garden. So thanks very much, and come next spring, I'll be back in that nice box you put up and get some more eggs to hatch.

Well, I'm off now. Thanks for listening, but then you've got class, I mean, I was the best, wasn't I? Worth waiting for? Worth having in *your* garden? Hmmmm? Oh, I near-ly forgot - some of you hoomans keep

# CATS!

Well, if you do, and you want to have us pop stars in the garden, better put a little bell round their necks. Nothing more yucky than a pet cat with one of us in its mouth. I mean... well... ouch! Bye...

ZZZZZZzzZZZzzzZZZZZZZzzzzZzzzzzip!

*Part Three*
Woodland Birds

Wilfred the Woodpigeon

## Wilfred the Woodpigeon

*Skrmm... chu nnft... skrummmmm... chmmmm... skrmm-mm...* sorry... I know it's rude to talk with my mouth full, but I hadn't realised that I was on, you see. That's the problem with being a woodpigeon, hardly ever have a beak without grub stuffed in it! Got to keep my weight up see, can't afford to slim at all. Never know when the food supply is going to give up!

So what's going on then? What's the scene, folks? Oh, you want to hear all about us woodies, eh? I wish someone had told *me* about this! What do you mean, someone *did*? *Grunge-grimp-grottle*! Me and my memory! In one birdie ear and out of the other, that's me. Can't even remember what time of the day it is sometimes. Well, why should I? The sun comes up, the sun goes down, sometimes it's wet and sometimes it isn't, warm or cold. That's all I care about!

Well, I'm not loafing around here for long. Sorry, but my tummy would never stand for it. I'm hungry right now. I was hungry when the sun came up, and I'll *still* be hungry when the sun goes down, that's a fact! I've been hungry for as long as I can remember, which isn't very long I admit. All I can remember is that I've always been hungry. Best dreams that I have are of great big fields full of corn seeds or lots of lush new green shoots to pick.

In fact, the *best* dream of all is of my lying on my satin-grey back, with my bill open, and a great big seed-fall of corn, just dropping straight down my gullet! Oh yesssssss! Wonderful that. I don't care about my waist-line, I don't have one anyway! I never seem to get too fat to fly, and that's all that matters. And I don't care that my tummy makes me steal some of your hooman food in the fields. You shouldn't leave it there, it's so tempting you know with a tummy growling like a trickling stream!

What a sacrifice I made, just being here, talking to you. There's my woodie buddies in that cornfield just over there, stuffing their beaks for all they're worth, and here's me, just cooing to you lot! You'd better make it worth my while, and let me have a go in your bean patch afterwards. I can see those lines of fresh bean shoots off in no time and *still* be hungry.

I'm a bit worried about why I should be here with all the woodland birds in any case. Which of you hoomans decided to call us woodies or woodpigeons? Well, I'm glad it wasn't you! Hey, mind if I ask you a question? Why *do* you give us such funny names, anyway? Come on now, own up. Well, why? Oh... I see... you call me a pigeon because I'm a fairly big grey bird? Hey, wait a minute, Herbie heron is a big grey bird, and you don't call *him* a pigeon, now do you?

Oh right, he is much bigger than me, and yes, you are right, he does have legs as long as ladders and a neck to go with it. Oh... right... we pigeons are all about the same size with the same kinds of heads and beaks... and we sound alike, eh? Hmm... I hadn't thought of that. You hoomans are quite right, we pigeons *do* sound rather alike, I admit. I mean, those blinking collared doves, sound a bit like us, even if they are doves and not pigeons, which is to say they are a little bit smaller and slimmer. So far as I am concerned, doves are pigeons, so don't try to make me believe anything different, okay?

I don't even know why I am bothering to talk to you! You hoomans seem to spend a lot of time walking about with those thin fire sticks that go bang, and make us drop out of the sky and off our twigs. And then, you have that really disgusting habit of plucking our feathers and cooking us. Oh Gaia! You are worse than buzzards and hawks. At least they don't stick us in ovens and then cover us with yucky brown sticky stuff, and nosh us with mashed potatoes! And for Gaia's sake, stop putting those strings of banging twigs in the fields where we eat. They scare the feathers off me, I can tell you. It's not like we eat the lot, you know, I mean, we leave you lot a few bits!

Where was I? Remind me? Oh right, yes, doves... collared doves. Well, who brought them here? What? You used to keep them in cages and one day, *you let them out*? Well, I thought you hoomans had more sense. You should have known that those pesky collared doves would breed like pigeons! They're everywhere, *coo-HOOO-hooo-hooo-hoo*. What a beak! Yes, everywhere!

As a matter of fact, collared doves are quite nice to look at, even if they *are* a pain in the fluff. Nice grey bodies, with little black collars, but not so nice as *my* collar! My collar is spotted with snow-white and bright green feathers, with a nice blush of purple. Now beat that! And my bill is very colourful too. Pink as pink, with a little dab of white. And I reckon my eyes are much more cute than theirs. Of course there are stock doves, and they are a lot like us to look at, except round their necks and the way they fly. Stock doves always seem to be in a hurry, flying as straight as an arrow, with regular nervy wing beats.

Now, I fly with a nice relaxed style, nice and cool, nice and calm. Except when I get in a flap about something, like one of you hoomans with a fire stick, or a fox. Then I take off and flap a few quiet flaps, then some real big noisy ones... yessss! To tell you the truth, I haven't got a clue as to how I make that clapping sound. Sometimes it feels like my wings slap together, and sometimes I feel like my wing tips crack like a flicked whip. Ah well, got to keep you hoomans guessing, I guess! Then I glide real quiet like, drifting down a little, then some more quiet flaps and some more loud claps.  All the lady woodies like that sound too.

I know you hoomans keep pigeons as pets.  Can't think why.  Some of 'em look ridiculous, especially those ones that are white or look like coloured sweets with outrageous crests and bent wing feathers and odd-looking tails. Personally, I reckon they are just a bunch of swanks, all flash and charm.  My Gaia, you even race them!  Well, you can keep all those daft fantails, and racing pigeons.  I reckon they give us woodies a bad name.

Now, we woodies are fantastic.  Very sociable and matey too.  Nothing better than feeding in a big field in great big bunches of grey sleek blobs, noshing amongst the freshly sown brown earth or on golden carpets of corn stubble... *coo-hoo-hoo-hoo-hoo*... aren't I a poet?

Now, when it comes to nesting time, I don't care where I nest, so long as it's in a nice big tree or bush, with plenty of leafy curtains drawn, just in case, like!  It's kinda odd, but I don't know many birds that like to make a nest in public.  Embarrassing and dangerous, that's what I think.  And you know, I really *can't* understand the fuss some birds make about making a nest.  Last year, my mate Wilma and me built a nest in a great big laurel bush.  Oh, I know it's not a native tree, it's one you hoomans brought here from somewhere else, but it suited us just fine.

We grabbed heaps of little dead twigs from all over the place, and just made a nice flat platform of them, criss-crossing them neatly and about the same size as one of your hooman dinner plates.

Great fun dating lady woodies.  Great time to use my neck muscles, I can tell you!  Yep - bobbing and tangoing all over the place, strutting the light fantastic for sure.  I *coo* and *noodle*, and putt my chest feathers out, and do a little bit of kissing and cuddling with my bill and neck.  Well, Gaia, the woodie ladies love it.

Got confusing last spring though. There was this other woodie guy, Wally by name. I mean, what a silly name! And what a cheek, having a name that sounds so much like mine. But I soon sorted him out! A quick session of bashing about in the bushes, wings flashing and smashing, and he was off!

Wilma laid the best-looking pair of pearly white eggs I have ever seen. Don't tell her this, but I really get a lump in my gizzard when the chicks hatch. Oh Gaia, are they *ugly*! Pink and floppy, heads lolloping all over the place, bumping into things 'cos they can't see, and making such a mess, oh my! But after a few sunrises, they started to feather-up nicely, and before you know it, they've got a nice set of grey feathers, and start to look... well... how can I put it? Respectable! Nothing worse in my bird book, than a badly dressed woodie. Lets the side down, I reckon!

It's a bit of a worry during this time. Too many big mouths around, just waiting for a fat woodie chick for lunch. That's why we try to hide the nest, see? I can remember the first time I flew, I mean, oh Gaia, it's a long drop if you get things wrong. Me? Well, I just kind of got the courage to leap off the nest, and hoped for the best. I can't say I *flew* out of the nest first time, more like fell out of it. Thank goodness, I'd done my practice in the nest. Heaps of flapping up and down, so I was okay.

Well, my tummy is growling, so I'd better be off now. I reckon I just broke a record here. Can't remember spending so much time cooing and not eating! Nice to see you here. Bye now!

Caroline the Cuckoo

## Caroline the Cuckoo

*Gnar twombo tooa dana meeta keear.* Oops! Sorry! I forgot to speak in English! See, it's like this, I'm pretty smart as birds go. Not many of us are bilingual, but I am! I live in Africa for at least half the year, when you hoomans have your cold months. Nice and warm down there. Lots of lovely food there too.

Hey, anybody watching? You will tell me if there is anyone listening or looking won't you? Are you *sure* there's no one else here? Sure? *Quite sure?* Okay, I believe you. Gotta be careful, most birds here don't seem to like us cuckoos being about.

Funny that. Look, I know this might offend you, but I simply *must* just check to make sure that we are alone - okay, the place looks clear. I guess I should have known that. If there *were* sneaky birds about, they'd be clattering and chattering all over the place. I get offended every time it happens, those meanies, they treat us cuckoos just like they do owls and hawks and that. Gangs of them, screaming and shouting at us!

Why? Search me! What do you mean, *I look like a hawk*? What? Is that true? Oh well, I guess you are right there. Yep, we do have long sleek bodies, with long tails all barred with black stripes and white spots, and okay, it's a fair comment, we do fly a lot like hawks; pointed wings, smooth firm flight. So what? Are they blind or what? And yes, we do seem in a hurry when we are flying. Well, I mean, we *are* in a hurry! If you got mobbed and shouted at every time you showed yourself in a hooman street, *you'd* keep moving pretty quick, wouldn't you?

What was that? No, over there. I thought I saw a bird in that bush - no - over there, silly. Are you sure? Nothing? Well, keep your eyes open and warn me if one of 'em sneaks up on us, okay?

I like the name you hoomans have given us, kind of respectful. Shows you hoomans listen too. I mean my name is pretty well *exactly* the same sound as my daddy cuckoo partners make. Yes, the guys do all the cuckoos. Me? I just chatter and laugh a lot, got a good sense of humour, see. Well, you've got to if you are a bit sneaky like me! Helps to make things cheerful and fun.

Oh, you've noticed? Yep, I'm as brown as a conker. All speckled, but brown just the same. Okay, some of us cuckoo gals *are* sometimes grey, but that ain't common over here in Britain. No, chances are when you see a grey cuckoo, it's a fella!

*Shhhhh! Listen!* Oh, just a bit of wind moving that willow tree. Thought it was a blackbird for a mo'. *Clik-clik-Clik... yacketty-yack* they go, whenever they get a sight of us cuckoos. A real pain in the fluff they are. Why can't they mind their own business?

It's not like we cuckoos are nasty or anything, now is it? You hoomans like us, so what's the problem with all these birdie mobsters? Ya know, you've got me a bit baffled here. I mean, why did I have to speak now, with all these woodland birds? I don't like thick woods. I don't know many cuckoos who do. Oh, I see. Got it, well, yes, we do llike wooded areas. Yep, that's true.

Remember, I told you we fly all the way from Africa each year? You knew that? Oh, I see. Well, I bet you don't know how we find our way? No, sillies, we don't have maps! And there ain't no signposts either - you know, great big posters saying 'Cuckoo M5 - turn left for England'. *Gratta-gratta-ubble-ubble...* sorry. Couldn't help having a little bubbly chuckle at that joke! This big journey we make, flying to come and nest here, that's got a real BIG name, that you hoomans have thought up.

Migration. Yes, that's it, migration. Means... to move about I think... or go from one place to another.

Now I don't like this habit you hoomans have of calling your birds *resident* or *visitors* or *migrants*! You got a problem with me visiting from Africa? Oh well, it's a habit you've got I guess. Like to put labels on things, eh? Well plumage yourselves. Yep, we ain't got no maps, but as sure as a cuckoo, we find our way there - come black time or light time. Come fog or rain. Our Ambassador here told us that you hoomans have had problems working out how we migrate. Well... tough!

I don't know about these things, honestly! It's just that we *know* where to go, and when. If ya like, the best way to say this is that we have a *programme* in our heads that tunes in to the directions we have to follow. I know that doesn't help much, but hey! How do you hoomans know how to find your way home? Mostly we fly back here alone or in ones or twos. Don't know why that is, just goes that way I guess.

When we get here, we go back to the patches where we were born, and just skoot about listening a lot. My mate last year, was a really nice cockoo, he called my name so sweetly. Couldn't resist a date or two with him! He was good at song fights too. Oh yeah! We cuckoos settle our differences with a nice noisy scrap. Cuthbert, my hubbie, used to sit in a tree, and if any other naughty cuckoo guy so much as stuck a beak too near our patch he'd open his mouth, stretch out his wings like your hoomans' Batman, and yell! Worked a treat.

Next job was mine actually. See, it's like this, we don't build nests...

Shhh! Hey! Duck down a second - hide! Keep quiet and very still... there's a blackbird hanging around over there... sh! wait, I don't want to be seen... oh wait, he's gone... cuc-phew! What a relief!

Oh yeah, we don't build nests. Waste of time if you ask me! Nope, we just look for another bird's nest, and use that. Well, I guess I'd better tell you the whole story.

There are over one hundred different kinds of birds that we use to help us raise our babies. How nice of them! Now me, I like to lay my eggs in hedge sparrows' or black-birds' nests. They fit my fluffy bottom so well, though I reckon hedge sparrows could be a bit more obliging and make them just a bit bigger. I have to squat over the top of the little cup nest, and try to get my aim right. Some of my sisters even lay eggs in nests in holes in trees and walls. This must be brilliant! Can't think how they do it, the eggs must fire out like rockets. I'd miss by a lot of wing flaps if I tried it!

Right, so I look for a blackbird's nest, see, and wait until they have finished building and laid their eggs. Then I sneak down and drop a single egg in with the others. I do hope you hoomans aren't a little squeamish, the next bit's a little yucky - if you are a bit... how shall I say this ... *sensitive*. Well, you may well wonder how a bird as big as me could lay an egg that would fool a blackbird, never mind something even smaller, like a hedge sparrow.

Now this is a bit sneaky I know, but we cuckoos seem to have a real special talent for copying other bird's eggs. Neat, eh? We can even adjust the size to suit the nest! So I lay an egg that looks as much like the others as possible, and do you know what? It works! Oh... *kre-kre-kre-kre-kre-kre!* Yep, they don't seem to get it, just go about their birdie business as usual. And here's another bit of cuck-cleverness; if the others' eggs hatch out first, it makes no difference. Once my darling little cuck-baby has hatched... it just starts to... well... have you guessed yet? Hmmmm... no? Well, the little darling gets the other chicks lined up right between its little pink featherless wings and heaves and heaves, and pushes and pushes, until the other chicks are tumbled right out of the nest! If there are eggs there, no problem, easier in fact. Out they go, the lot of them.

Now, I know you might not approve of that and it might give us cuckoos a bad name, but there it is. Don't blame me. It's all Gaia's idea. In the long-flap, it's kinder, after all my chick's going to get *really* big, and there wouldn't be room for the others in the nest. Why the blackbirds don't get wise and chuck my little darling out, I don't know. Must be something to do with them being parents, I guess.

So you see, we cuckoos might like making baby cuckoos, but don't expect me to go all soft and gooey about feeding them, 'cos I won't. I just lay away, and leave it to the oh-so-nice foster birds to do the hard bit, okay? Shhh... whoops - are you sure that blackbird over there isn't spying on us? Sure? You won't tell them about this will you... promise? It's only natural you know.

Yep, if you are lucky, come the early summer, you can spy out one of our little baby cuckoo darlings sitting in a nest. I've got to confess that I have to chuckle every time I see it! I mean, have you ever thought what it would be like for one of your hooman grown-ups to get back into one of those funny wheely things you take *your* babies round in? *Ke-ch-ke-ch-ke-ch-ke-ch!* Oh, what a laugh. Actually, sitting *in* the nest isn't half of it, more like sitting round the nest! Now it's not so bad seeing blackbirds feeding a cuck-chick, they are almost the same size you see. But the sight of a hedge sparrow, no bigger than my head and neck in size, feeding a great big fat brown fluffy cuck-chick has me in stitches! I don't know why those foster birds don't get wise! You would think that they would notice the fact that their little darling is three times bigger than them, wouldn't you?

Maybe they say to each other, 'Wow! what *have* we been feeding this guy? Must be a new kind of worm or grub that makes him *that* big. Go on like this, and the little darling will explode!' Of course, the little darling doesn't explode, it just goes on getting bigger and bigger intil it's ready to fly. Last year, I saw a pair of hedge sparrows feeding a cuck-chick that was so big, they had to sit on its back to stuff its beak full of food!

Now I've been looking at you hoomans a lot. Seems to me that you aren't much like us birds, except that you walk on two legs like we do. I mean, you've got things that look like they should be wings, but you don't try to fly with them. Odd that, but I'm smart, I've worked it out. You *couldn't* fly with wings that small, and you'd need muscles as big as your whole bodies to get off the ground too. You're too heavy see, and anyway, you haven't got feathers now have you?

And another thing, you hoomans don't have tails - at least I don't *think* you do - but perhaps you keep them wrapped up inside your plumage trousers or skirts? Don't get me wrong, we don't really have tails, well, not like foxes do. We have tail *feathers*. In my case, my tail feathers are just about as long as my body. Our tails help us to steer when we fly - we can twist them and turn them, and they help us to change direction, to go up and down, and to keep balanced. Neat, eh?

And, hey, I'm *not* deaf! All birds have ears, it's just that they can't normally see them. In Africa, there are some rather weird-looking birds that have much yuckier habits than we do. They fly around eating dead animals and rotting flesh. Well! I mean! Well, these birds are vultures see, and they don't have feathers on their heads. Well, not many. Now I don't recommend this, but if you were silly enough to take a close look (hold your nose, oh Gaia, have they got bad breath) you could actually see the little holes just back from their eyes. These holes are birdie ears. Okay?

I've noticed that some owls have little tufts of feathers that grow right out from their ear-holes, and I believe you have two owls here that actually have the word 'eared' in their names? What was it? Oh yes, I remember, long and short-eared owls, yes, that's it.

My ears are hidden under the feathers of my head, just back from my eyes, and don't worry, I can hear just fine, and so can all the other birds too. I'm not saying that I can hear as well as owls, but I can hear really well, believe me.

And yes, we can smell things through our beaks and... shhhh... keep still... see that? That rotten blackbird has been and grassed on me, now there's two more of 'em... clicking away and staring at me... and now there's a thrush turned up as well... and some sparrows... oh, what a pain... can't get any peace round here. Well, I know when I'm not wanted and anyway, I was ready to fly off. Don't go looking for me when summer's full on because I'll be on my way back to Africa, okay? Oh no - more of 'em turning up... and all pointing and staring at me... and yelling rude things... I'm outta here. Cuckbye!

Gazza the Green Woodpecker

## Gazza the Green Woodpecker

**Yak Yak Yak** Yak Yak Yak Yak Yak Yak Yak
Yak! Yeeaah! Oh yeah, great, mate! Man, what a buzz!
Yaffling, I mean yip! Yaffling, that's what I like. Nothing
better than a good yaffle to get the blood trilling. Some
disrespectful yobbos say that we are all chatter and no
sense, but I don't agree. Okay, I might seem a bit crazy
sometimes, ya know, a bit soft in the head, but hey, *you'd*
be a bit soft in the head if you banged your head against
things as many times as I do, especially in the spring!

I dunno what comes over me. Just can't resist finding a
nice big hollow log or tree and, well, just bang my bill into
it, really hard, and as fast as I can. Great fun, I can tell
you. Trouble is, all that head banging kinda affects my
poor brain, right? I get sort of dizzy and silly, the wood
spins around like one of your hooman tops, ya know?

Thank Gaia, she's given me a really nice cushion
between my bill and my brain, so things don't get too bad.
You know, it's kinda like a shock absorber. What? You
don't know what a shock absorber is? Well, you try banging your head against a wall, but MAKE SURE that you put
a pillow there first. Well, the pillow is the shock absorber,
got it? So right, I like head banging. Well, that's okay, isn't
it? Mind you, it's got to be a dead hollow piece of wood,
makes much more noise see?

You hoomans have drums, right? Well, they ain't solid
are they? Nope! Best drums for me are hollow ones.
Why do I do that head banging? Silly! I like to score,
okay? Don't be daft, not one of your hooman footy goals.
I mean score with the lady 'peckers, got it? Yip! Ya got it.
I drum 'cos it turns the ladies on, you wouldn't believe how
much! Now, I know you hoomans have got big ears, but

I'll bet you didn't realise that we green woodpeckers all have our own special drum breaks! Hey, come on now, I mean, where do you hoomans live? Some of you guys have got those funny plastic things with wires coming out of them right? Ya know, you talk in them, and some other hooman at the other end says 'hello, who's that there?' Yip, phone, that's right - phone. Well, you've got phone numbers right? What's the first bit called? *Area code*, oh right! Then what? Yip, you are smart. Then you've got your own number. Right on!

Well, the noise we make is like our area code, see? then each head-banger beats a special number of beats, special speeds and numbers of bangs. No I ain't giving you my number, so there! Well, if you *really* want to know, I do eighteen bangs in less than a second. Beat that! Wow, what a joke. Got it? *Beat that*! Yek-yek-yek!

So, ya see, the 'pecker chicks have got my number, oh man! I know what turns 'em on see. Best drummer gets the chick.

The other thing is that the other local head bangers get kinda turned off when they hear me drum! Well, they do if they get too close. So ya know, this is great - we settle our differences with a little head banging all on our own. No need to get rough, if ya know what I mean. During the spring, hardly ever see another guy, I can *hear* 'em though. I'm just not stupid enough to flip on over and get too close.

Now, get a load of this, take a good look at my feathers! Great, eh? Green as oak leaves, and what a red hat, eh? Nice little black chin under my bill, and man - check my eyes out! Yip, nearly as white as white - well... a very pale grey anyway. Almost the colour of that pale honey you hoomans seem to like. Ain't my tail neat too? Nice point-ed black feathers, and the greatest splash of bright yellow... oh man... I'm handsome!

And try this one, most of the birds you've been talking to have got feet like mine, only they point three toes forward and one toe back. You knew that didn't you? Well, I point *two* toes forward and *two* back. Guess why. How are you doin'? Well, where do I do most of my walking? Yip, you got it, up and down trees, right! Not many birds walk up and down things as near straight as one of your hooman rulers, but we do. So we points our toes two-by-two to help us keep steady as we climb and drop down the tree trunks and branches.

Yeeeah! And I use my long strong tail to help support my weight see? I just press it towards the bark on the tree, and it keeps me there just fine. Apart from being the best-looking fella in the woods, I've got a few other things a lot of birds haven't. Well, better not boast too much, but man-oh-man you should just take a look at my tongue! You ain't gonna find many birds with a longer one, that's for sure. Now, I reckon that I've got a long bill, but when I stick my tongue out, it's enormous, yip, even longer than my bill.

Why? Noshing, that's why. Oh you didn't know? Yip - I eat one thing more than anything else and I'll bet you can't guess what that is. Try! Nope! WRONG! Think small little things with six legs that scuttle about in the grass, that rush about under stones, that build little mounds of earth to live in, or great mountains of pine nee-dles and twigs in the woods. Got it? These little critters sting too, and my can they bite. They live in great big bunches of 'em, sometimes thousands and thousands and hey, they are usually black or reddy brown... phew - at last. You got it - yip! Ants!

Well, ants live just about everywhere, but I'm sorry to say that they seem to keep on hiding under things, or deep inside stones and pieces of bark. What a pain. But it ain't no good, once we 'peckers get a whiff of these ants, we dig away with our bills and then stick our long tongues in the hole and 'sticky' 'em out! Yip, my tongue is covered with sticky stuff that sticks to the ants and their oh-so-yummy eggs. Then it's a quick gobble and they're gone.

Sometimes the little demons gang up on me though, stream up my legs like an angry army. That's when I start a tango man, do the bebop. Yeah! Shake 'em off quick, man can they bite!

I don't reckon this is very clever meself, but some 'peckers will even have a go at a wasps' nest. Now I ask you, how daft can you get? You can keep your wasps, so there. It's not worth the pain. Mind you, our feathers make it real hard for them wasp stings to get through. Thank Gaia!

I don't say no to the odd beetle mind, flies, woodlice and such like, and once I even tried to eat some pine seeds, but they were really grotty if you ask me. Nope - a good nosh on ants is best. I've been know to eat as many as a thousand in only a few minutes. Now you try stuffing a thousand biscuits into you in a few minutes, eh? Oh, they wouldn't fit? Oh, right on!

I like woods. Great spot to live in. Full of trees, you see! I don't just fly around in the woods though. Any place where there are ants will suit me fine. You know, I do realise that it's sometimes hard for you hoomans to know exactly what bird you are looking at. I mean, we don't exactly sit on your sitting room seat, and just wait for you to work out what we are, now do we? Well, there ain't many birds that are green like me. I... well... yes, I know about green finches, I mean, they are green too, but you know, I'm three times bigger than them, and I have a red hat, see!

And if you don't mind my making a couple of suggestions: for starters, I fly in a very special way, kinda straight but with a real up and down drift, if you get my drift! We kinda look like we are going up and down on a gentle roller coaster. Now, I know that there are other birds that fly a bit like that, but if you see a big green bird doing that in a park or field near woods, chances are that you'll get top marks in identification, clever you!

And ya know, most birds have voices that are pretty easy to recognise. You couldn't mistake my *yak-yak-yak-yak*, and I'm a head banger remember, so that narrows things down a bit. I have some cousins though, but they're smaller than me and black and white, with red bits on their heads and throats. They look like they've got white measles. So I guess that's why you hoomans call them spotted woodpeckers. They fly a lot like me, and they are pretty cute at head banging too.

Hang on! There's another one! Over there, can't you hear him? He's banging away on a tree on the far side of the wood. I know him, it's Graham. He's one of us, but a bit of a nuisance. If I don't go and start some headbanging soon, he'll attract the most sexy lady, and I'll miss out on the fun. I'll be back in a minute, just got to do a quick sesh with the old hollow piece of beech wood I chose as my drum. Be right back.

*taka taka taka taka taka taka taka taka!*

Oh man! That hurt, my head's spinning, the world's going round and round, and your face is going up and down like crazy. Keep still will you, stop jumping up and down like that! Oh man, this is weird. Happens every time I do this. Everything is a bit hazy and blurred. Nice feeling, but I *do* wish you'd settle down. Looks to me like you've got about thirty faces there!

Well, I think I'm in here, there's a lovely lady greenie sitting right over there behind me. She says her name is Geraldine, nice name, nice lady. Oh man, I think I'm in here! I'd like a date with her. In a minute, I'm gonna go right back, and take her to the tree I've chosen for a nest. Most of the work is already done. I think I may have used that nice deep hole in that oak tree last year, I just can't remember right now, my head's still spinning.

Yip! I'll hop up in the tree, and do some fancy head drawing. Oh come on! *Head drawing*? Yeah, imagine my beak as a pencil. Well, I make these nice shapes in the air with it round and round, nice big loops and that. The ladies just *adore* it! If I really *am* in there, that Geraldine chick will be just great! We'll finish cleaning out the nest hole, ya know, dig some more of the dead wood out, make a nice deep tunnel inside. We leave a nice soft pile of wood chips in the bottom, and if I'm lucky, this Geraldine chick will lay as many as six or seven eggs in there. Nice white ones, almost round, 'cos they fit nicely, being round.

I've got a confession to make, okay? We greenies do sometimes get a bit rough if another fella is silly enough to get too close. Usually it's just a lot of bashing around with our wings, especially when chasing each other, and not much harm done, but I have heard rumours of things getting really nasty, and one of my buddies was killed in a fight last year. What a waste of life. I guess Gaia knows what she's doing, but I hope it doesn't happen to me.

No, give me a nest full of little darlin's and I'm happy. Hard work though. Do you hoomans eat all day? No? Well you can come and sit on my nest any day! My chicks last year were hungry from sunrise to sunset. What a relief when they shut up for the night and slept! For more than three weeks, my lady and me had to fly back and forth into that hole and just stuff the little darlin's! I didn't even have much time to get into some head banging!

Then they got big enough to stick their beaks out of the nest hole, and instead of yelling for nosh from inside... they stuck their beaks out and yelled outside! Embarrassing, I mean, well, hey, bird-folks might get the idea that my lady and me were lazy or something.

Thank Gaia, the magic day always comes when the little sweeties launch out of the nest hole and take their first flight. Usually my lady and me take them to the best noshing places, ya know, give them a bit of a claw in learning how to eat for themselves. Then things go a lot quieter. We grown-ups get some rest, and wait for the cold breath of the autumn winds to come sneaking in.

Nothing more scary than a cold winter to us 'peckers. A real bad one can see a lot of us flitting off to birdie heaven, if you get my meaning. That's when I might pluck up the courage to make a visit to your garden, and even sneak a little bit of food from your bird tables. So nice of you hoomans to do that, has anybody thanked you for that?

Well, my head's feeling a lot better now, and I can see that you've stopped moving up and down. Wow! That Geraldine chick is a good-looker! Yip, I know she looks just like me, but hey, I can tell she's a girl 'cos she ain't behaving like a guy, okay? Well, friends, I gotto go to do a bit of showing off. If she really likes me, she might let me chase her up and down that beech tree, and if I *really* am in there, she might even let me have a little snog with my beak and hers. Oh man! I've been yacking here long enough! I'm looping off now, Bye!

# Yak-yak-yak-yak-yak-yak-yak...

Betty the Bullfinch

# Betty the Bullfinch

Stay right where you are! Right there - you hear me? No? Not loud enough? I can't help that... listen! Stay there, don't come any nearer - come any nearer and I'm off... right?... promise? You won't come any nearer..? okay then... I'll talk to you then... keep still... don't move... quite still... you scare me if you move...

I'm sorry, but I'm really shy, honestly I am. Very shy. Can't help it, it's in my nature. Oh yes, I know I'm a big finch, but that doesn't count. Some finches are not shy, and some are. You are lucky to see me at all, and that's a fact. If I was a haw finch, you'd probably never see me at all. You'll just have to accept that I don't like being looked at much, okay?

Yes, you could try sneaking up on me, when I'm busy eating. I probably wouldn't notice you, if you're good at that, but if you make a sound, if you make a sudden movement, I'm off, okay? That's what comes of being a small bird. Small bird - easy to eat! You could fit me in your hand easily, but you'd better not try, I can bite! I couldn't help noticing that you just had a twitter and yacker with Gazza. Well, he's a bit of a nutter, I think!

No silly! I don't mean he eats nuts, *we* eat nuts, well, seeds mainly. That's why I have such a heavy and solid bill. Yes, just look at it - NO, don't come any closer! That's close enough, you can see what a big bill I have from where you are. Talking of nutters, I guess we bullfinches do have something in common with woodpeckers. We like woods too, and we have nice colours too, not like Gazza though - he has a nice red cap, and we have nice black caps, black as coal, black as night, black as black!

Now take my mate Bertie - no, not that one - that's a chaffinch - I mean that handsome cute bird over there in that wild cherry tree, yes, the one with the nice pearly white blossoms on it. See? Yes, lovely bright pink body with a back as grey as wood ashes, same colour on the back as the back of a donkey.

Well, compare him to me. I'm almost the same as him except that I'm greyer all over, a little bit of pinky colour on my chest, and my back is a little bit browner than his.

Otherwise, we both have black caps, black wings and a nice black tail. We both have a little white bar on our wings, and a lovely white bit round our... well... round our bottoms if that's not rude to admit. When we fly, we show off that white flash at the back, and our black wings go all blurred with black and white, please try to remember that!

I'm sorry about this being shy bit, can't help it. I like to keep in good cover myself, nice thick patches of twigs and leaves. That's why I like the woods. And don't go expecting to see me eating on the ground, because that's not going to be something you'll see very often. I like to eat well off the ground, where there are nice bits of fruity seeds to eat. I like yew berries and holly berries, love the red berries on mountain ash. Anything that has a nice juicy skin with seeds inside.

I also adore fresh shoots in trees and shrubs, and to be honest with you, this gets us bullfinches into a spot of bother with you hoomans. I mean, take my mate Bertie over there, he's busy eating wild cherry buds. We loooove cherry buds, apple buds, plum buds, pear buds... oh, yummeeeee! Bertie has just eaten more than thirty buds in as long as it takes you to say, 'Hey, I wonder what that bird is doing in that tree over there? It seems to have a real cheek, eating all those fresh shoots. The fruit farmer is not going to be very happy about that.'

That's why you hoomans put those banging things in your cherry orchards, and why you used to kill us with those spitting fire stick things. Hey, that's not fair - we have to eat as well as you, you know! No wonder we are so shy. And another thing, if you were as brightly coloured as we are, you'd try to keep out of sight too wouldn't you? Well you would if nasty sparrowhawks and buzzards liked to eat you, which I am sorry to say, in our case, happens to be true!

It's hard to accept, but things eat *us* just like we eat things. It's just that we eat mainly plants, but some others eat animals. This is why you hoomans call us *herbivores*, whilst other birds are called *carnivores*. The carnivores eat animals and the herbivores eat plants, interesting isn't it? I believe some of you hoomans are vegetarians? Well, join the bullfinch club if you are! Okay, in nesting time, we tend to change our habits a bit, and feed the babies with grubs and things, but for most of the year we are vegetarians, and that's the truth.

Now you don't often see bullfinches in gangs. Oh yes, it's true that we gather in flocks in the winter, but even that's unusual, and we seldom get into gangs of more than a half dozen or so. Bertie and me get on so well that we stick together for the whole time. It's very rare to hear of bullfinches getting divorced. Most other finches don't get married. They just start dating again each spring. I don't know how they cope, I can't be bothered myself and anyway, Bertie is cute and cuddly, and he sticks with me, and I stick with him.

I'm not all that bright, I guess, but I reckon this is why we don't sing all that much, and what's nicer, I reckon this is why both daddy and mummy bullfinches sing! Nothing fancy mind, mainly just a single little *pheew*, with the little song tipping down at the end, like the end bit has a little weight on it to drag it down ever so slightly.

This has got to be good news for you hoomans. I know you like to hear birds sing, and we get complaints about packing up singing in the winter. Well, not us bullfinches!

We sing all year round. So be grateful, and thank us, okay?

Do you mind if I ask you to do something for me? NO! Don't come any closer! Just stay where you are, I can see fine thanks. Well, would you mind just opening your mouth nice and wide? Wider please, I want to see inside. Hmmmmm... interesting... I can see now that you hoomans eat both vegetables and meat. Yes, it's those teeth you have. Some for tearing and some for chewing. Well, you can tell what birds eat in the same way: pointed beaks are usually for snapping insects, or spearing fish, flat ones for dabbling in water, hooked ones for tearing flesh and fat thick ones for breaking seeds open. Got that? Just trying to help here!

Don't try to find my nest next year. I'm jolly good at hiding it. The neatest little bowl of tiny twigs and woven grasses, lined with the softest little strands of grass that we can find. I laid six eggs last spring. I don't usually lay more than that, unless something terrible happens to the nest, then we have to start again.

It took a lot of courage for me to come and twitter with you. I'm so shy. Please remember to keep your distance. Just because I'm such a bold-coloured bird, it doesn't mean that I'm bold myself! I *do* hope I haven't bored you. I'm not very good at jokes, not like some birds I could mention! Well, see you around, I expect - just make sure that you stay right over there right? Right!

Jimmy the Jay

# Jimmy the Jay

nnnnnnnnnnnnnnnnnnnnnnnnnnnnneeeeeeeow!

Ooo, my dearies, what fun! There oy was, sittin' in the top of that oak tree, just watching yew and Betty bullfinch chatting, so oy just perched there and thought to moyself, *oy wonder what on earth they be screeching about*. Oy can't think of anything moyself. Bullfinches b'ain't much to talk to, neew be they?

Then oy sees that yew be finished loyk, so oy zooms down from the tree, stretchin' the ole' wings ewt, all still loyk, and 'ere oy be! Now oy knows my accent be a bit funnee loyk, well, oy be from Wiltshire see? But yew can foynd us jays about anywhere, anywhere where there be trees loyk, 'specially fir trees. Them's the best oy reckon, though oy loyk oak trees too.

Anyways, oy'm tryin' to say that yew can see jays loyk me all over the place. Woy, yew could go royt across to China and beyond and still see some of moy mates there! Jays is a big success story. We do well just about anywhere!

See, it's loyk this, we's big birds, well, fairly big anyway. About at as big as one of them jackdaws, and we eats anythin' at all and that 'elps, really it does. Yes 'oomans 'ave a good word for we birds what eat anythin', *omnivores*, yes, that be it, omnivores. Means that we eat both veggies and meat! Oy loyk acorns best moyself, but oy'll eat beetles, caterpillars, grubs, floys, nuts, seeds, little birds, moyce, the odd mole. Anythin' small enough to gobble in fact.

Screetchin' of jackdaws, boy the way, we jays be related to 'em, yew know? I means, we be members of the crow family, now ain't that queewt? Oy'm glad that oy'm so brightly coloured mind, them crows is nearly all black and oy reckon that's a shame, really oy does! Neew, take a look at me! Oy'm very noice to look at. Best set of black whiskers down my white chin, and oooh, moy spotted forehead. Noice one!

In fact, moy dears, there ain't a bit of me that b'ain't noyce to look at. Time was when yew 'oomans collected my feathers and stuck 'em in your hats, and that's a fact. Oy've got black wings moynd, and big whoyt bars on 'em, so when oy floys yew can see them black and whoyt feathers a flashin' loyk anythin'. Noice big black beak too, if oy may say so! Moy oys? Well neew, let me see... kina... pale they be... sort of grey and brewnish like. Charmin', that's what oy thinks.

Neew, oy reckon that some of these 'ere birds is a bit snobbish loyk. They don't loyk moy accent see, they reckons that oy'm kina rustic! *Rustic*? Well oy ask yers. Just 'cos oy dunt talk loyk them they gets all upperty and fluffed up. Loyk down their beaks at us jays they does, it ain't royt! I nose moy place I does, oy keeps moyself to moyself. In fact, I reckon as we jays is real noice like, it's just that we dunt gew flashing and swanking about loyk... weeeel... I s'pose we does screetch a lot... but we 'ave a great voice, yew nose! I dunt sound like a blackbird, but we makes a great noyse loyk a noyf bein' scraped on a stone, and me and moy mates can't half copy other birds. Oy can make a noise loyk a' owl. There b'ain't many sounds oys wouldn't troy given 'alf the chance.

We jays keeps to ourselves, like... oh well... yers...sometoyms we gets into little mobs... but that's the winter for yews. Cum the spring, we gets on our own, like, sittin' in tall trees, lookin' dewn on them fields and waitin' for a noyce laydee to floy by. Then, oy bobs and curtsies loyk, reaches ewt moy feathers and tilts moy 'ed forward and makes the best noises oy can think orv.

Then we goes, me and the missus, and foynds a noice big tree to get some twigs stuffed into, and makes sure that we ain't be so silly as to let the nest be seen too easy, 'specially from above. Warll! That'd be real stupid like. Neew I reckon we jays 'as got a lot a guts, oy mean, there ain't much we is scared orv. Take me neew, I ain't even scared if them black an yella floyin' things what makes that buzzin' noise, yew no, they 'as little stings in their tails, and they can give yew one moyty sting with 'em as well. Yep warsps that's it, warsps. Well, oy ain't scared to get into one of them papery nests and tear 'em to pieces, and eat whatever oy can get.

Well, me and the missus gets the nest ready. Then she lays abuwt four or foyve eggs, and that's that oy guess. Neew dunt yew troy to get near moy nest, yew'll get a nastee shock! Oy dunt like things near moy nest, so oy sits and screams, even gets to copy an 'awk or a buzzard yelling, just ta fool yew. An' if yew gets too close, oy'll even swoop dewn and flap moy wings at yew, so dew be careful. Oy even 'erd of a jay 'oo threw twigs dewn on to a fox beleew, so watch it!

Neew, oy dunt do the sittin' moyself, tend to leave that to the missus, but oy does 'elp build the nest, and feed the babbies, bless their little fluffy selves! Oy floys miles sometimes to get food. Come the winter, and oy gets 'eaps of acorns and stacks 'em away in a secret place loyk. Bit loyk a squirrel really, yew no, just stack 'em in a little crack in a tree, under some ferns, anywhere's secret. Saved moy loyf many a toym oy can tell yew.

Yew no oy was tellin' yew abewt yew 'oomans collecting our feathers? Well, some of moy cousins what lives in tewns and parks an' that, well, they've got used to yew 'oomans, and ain't 'arf as suspicious as what oy am.

Some of us even makes noice pets, but don't troy it, it ain't legal and yew'd get into a lot of trouble.

Well, there yew goes, that's about it really. Oy ain't dun bad neew 'ave I? Toym for me to flit orf oy reckons 'cos oy can see 'oo's next, and if there's one bird oy respects it's a' owl, specially the missus of the Ambassador for us birds. So oym orf. Take a look at my floyt, straight as oy can be, fast beats, 'eaps of black and whoyt and a noyce screech just to set your nerves on edge. Afternoon to yew awl! Funny old day, ain't it?

Tamsen the Tawney Owl

# Tamsen the Tawny Owl

How doo-hoo yoo-hoo doooooooo! My husband and I are so pleased too-hoo be here too-hoonight. I know that yoo-hoo hoomans have already met my husband, the Ambassador. I expect yoo-hoo realise that he and I live in the same neck of the woo-hoods as Herbie the heron? Well, that's not exactly true, yoo-hoo know. Herbie lives downriver from my husband and I, but we often see him flying up his beat on the river.

Yoo-hoo see, we live in the very top of a very tall larch tree, high above the little road that runs too-hoowards Buckfast Abbey. Oh, I know yoo-hoo might expect that we would have the Embassy in London, but yoo-hoo see, the job is only for two-hoo years, and it's our turn at the moment. Another tawny will take over next year, and I believe it is going too-hoo be Tessa in Suffolk next. Well, the hoo-hoot is that way, so I'm told.

It's quite right that my husband and I have been invited too-hoo talk as woo-hoodland birds, because most owls like woo-hoods. Our home here is among a stand of lofty larches, with many big sycamores behind us, and a great big cluster of old beeches between us and the river. During the daylight hours, we just perch in the shades of the branches, close too-hoo the rough brown trunk of the tree. Yoo-hoo woo-hood have a very hard time seeing us in the daytime, because we are so still, as still as statyoo-hoos, really!

It's a great honour too-hoo be working in the Embassy. There's so much work too-hoo be done yoo-hoo see. The biggest job we have too-hoo doo-hoo is too-hoo *think*. And that's why we tawnys spend so much time just sitting still. Well, I think it might be a goo-hood idea if I told yoo-hoo what a typical tawny day and night is like.

Well, take yesterday for example. My husband and I sat all day in the top of the same tree that I'm sitting in now. We normally use the same tree over and over again. Well, we have too-hoo really, otherwise nobody woo-hood know our address, now woo-hood they? We had spent the previous night hunting. Yoo-hoo must understand that in the bird world, things happen which might be a little shocking for yoo-hoo. Gaia has designed life so that we can all live too-hoogether in a world where things work out just fine, but that means that we doo-hoo things that... well... are not like what hoomans doo-hoo. At least, not nowadays!

Once, many moo-hoons ago, your hooman ancestors also went hunting, for wild animals, for berries and fruits, for fish and water. Now, most of yoo-hoo can get your foo-hood in shops and soo-hoopermarkets, so yoo-hoo don't need too-hoo hunt like we doo-hoo. Now, Gaia has given us owls wonderful sight and hearing. We can see things in the dark that yoo-hoo would never see. That's why our eyes are so big. Round each eye, we have a ring of feathers like a bowl. This allows us too-hoo focus sound on our faces so that our eyes go right too-hoo the spot where a sound comes from. Now, I know that some of yoo-hoo hoomans have television that comes from pictures that are sent from the sky. I believe you call this *satellite television*? Well, yoo-hoo have special round plates on your roo-hooves and walls to help you get the best picture, don't yoo-hoo? Yoo-hoo point the disc in the right direction too-hoo get the strongest signal, yes?

Our eye discs doo-hoo the same job, they magnify the sound, and our eyes can see where the sound of a scuttering mouse or dashing little rabbit, stirring in the inky darkness of night, comes from. We tawnys eat almost any small animal that we can find. I know this sounds very cruel, but we make sure that we kill our supper very quickly. Gaia has given us such strong beaks and claws, that we can kill even quite a big rabbit in a matter of seconds. Now of course, our bird relatives don't like being eaten, I can understand that, so when we are not on official doo-hooty like now, they make a lot of noise when they see us, and are not that polite either!

But I'm afraid it makes no difference. We have too-hoo eat, just like all birds doo-hoo. Now think about this, if we *all* ate the same things, there woo-hood not be enough too-hoo go around, now woo-hood there?

The easiest way too-hoo hunt is too-hoo sit still in a tree, close too-hoo some open ground, where we can see little animals dashing about. Then we drop like a stone from the sky, and pounce and kill. Gaia has given us owls very special wing feathers, which are so fine, so silky, that the wind does not make a sound as we fly throo-hoo the air. We are quite silent in the air. Aren't we lucky?

If we catch a big animal, like a small rabbit, my husband and I will sometimes share it. This is especially nice in the spring, because my husband likes too-hoo flatter me, and instead of bringing me a bunch of flowers or some perfume, he brings me a nice big fat mouse too-hoo eat. So sweet! Well, I was telling yoo-hoo that we both went hunting last night, flying sometimes too-hoogether, always calling too-hoo each other.

My husband shouts hoo, and I answer with a soft *keewik*. Now there is a funny thing. My husband was hoo-hooting with Edward Cowie about that, and he told my husband that yoo-hoo hoomans yoo-hoosed to think that this sound was made by one owl. Silly things! It's just my husband and I keeping in touch. We both like too-hoo fly zigzags all over our hunting grounds. We eat as much as we can each night, and then fly back too-hoo our high perch just before the sum comes up.

Now that's what we did last night. This morning, I just sat very quietly and let my tummy get too-hoo work on all that fur and bones. This is a little delicate for me to tell yoo-hoo because I'd hate for yoo-hoo too-hoo think that we owls had bad manners. But yoo-hoo see, we simply *can't* digest all those sharp little bones and all that cloggy fur. It's the same when we eat fish, which we doo-hoo sometimes, or big beetles with tough wing cases. Our owl tummies get too-hoo work, and make a little parcel of the bits our tummies can't cope with. Then in the daytime, I get that funny feeling in my tummy that yoo-hoo hoomans doo-hoo when yoo-hoo have eaten too-hoo much, or when yoo-hoo are on a boat on a rough sea.

Yes, my tummy gurgles and rumbles, and my throat starts to gulp and gag, and up it comes, a neat little package of fur, bones, scales, wing-cases. I cough a little of course, but it's no problem really and nobody is loo-hooking anyway! These little parcels of unwanted bits and pieces are called *pellets* by yoo-hoo hoomans, and it's by far the best way too-hoo discover where an owl roo-hoosts, too-hoo be honest.

Well, there yoo-hoo are, a typical tawny day and night. As I told yoo-hoo, my husband gets really fresh and attentive in spring though. We stay as mates for life, which is nice really and he is so attentive all the year throo-hoo. But in the spring, we find a nice big hole in a tree, scoo-hoop the dry woo-hood inside and make the hole deep enough too-hoo get inside and snuggle down in. Then I lay a few very round eggs, just like your hooman ping-pong balls, but a little smaller. Yoo-hoosually, I lay about four eggs. My husband stays nearby, and keeps guard, and woe betide any silly creature that comes between him and our nest! Then he will screech and scream and dive and flap and even scratch with his claws or bite with his sharp beak if he can. Isn't he wonderful? Well, I really must go now. Time flies and it's owls fly time. Time too-hoo drift along the meadows and find some foo-hood. Yoo-hoo have been *such* goo-hood listeners. Bye now.

*Part Four*
*Field Birds*

Ray the Rook

## Ray the Rook

W'hey! Me first, eh? Quite right too, I mean, putting *me* as the first field bird to talk to you hoomans! Oh Gaia, can I *caw*? I just love cawing, try stopping me. Life's a gas, really it is. So much going on, so much to caw about. Silent rooks are boring rooks in my feathery book. I never knew a rook worth knowing that didn't caw first and think afterwards!

Stands to reason, y'know. When you spend so much of your time living in a big crowd, if you don't caw a lot, it's bad news. The others will take advantage of you if you don't have your say. Now you know me, surely? What do you mean, you can't be sure when a rook is a rook? Come off it, are you really suggesting that we rooks look like any other birds? Oh, I see, well yes, I've got to admit that there are quite a lot of big black birds around. But let's get this straight right now, okay?

Rooks don't have the ash grey heads of jackdaws, and we aren't as big as crows or ravens, so there. And take a close look at my big strong beak. See what I mean? Yes, we have a big patch of whitish skin on the bill and round our eyes, kind of like we got carried away when shaving round our eyes and beak, if you know what I mean.

And another thing, when you see a big bunch of black birds standing in a field, well, they've got to be either rooks or jackdaws, and I've just told you that jackdaws are smaller and with grey heads, so let's not have any more of that silly nonsense about not recognising us rooks, okay?

We are a friendly lot normally, well, I think so anyway. Mind you, I've got to admit that I don't have the best temper around. Lots of things irritate me, get my feathers in a huff, if you know what I mean. Only yesterday a big bunch of us visited a big field to look for insects and seeds after the hooman farmer had been through on his big noisy thing with four round things to make it move. Well, I mean, now I don't mind crowds at all, love 'em in fact, but I do get awfully cross when other rooks get right up close and stick their bills into the same bit of ground that I have mine in!

Now I really can't stand that. There's heaps of room in that field see, and so why should another rook come and try to pinch *my* bit of field, eh? So, it's a matter of just getting all fluffed up, and hopping about a lot, wings waving about and snapping my beak and, well you've guessed it, *cawing*! Hey! There are times when it's really useful to caw at noshing time. I mean, all those little beetles and grubs don't exactly leap onto the ends of our bills and yell to be eaten, you know!

Many legs and bills make light work, that's what I say. So, get a big gang of about thirty or forty of us, and that's a *lot* of leg power. Must be like an earthquake when a big gang of rooks get stomping about in a field! You can't imagine how many yummy bugs make a dash for cover when we feed in gangs. And anyway, the best place to eat is where there's a crowd right? I mean, you hoomans would be a bit suspicious of going into one of your hooman cafes, if it was always empty now wouldn't you?

So yes, I fly around looking for a field of rooks, jackdaws or pigeons, 'cos they're just telling me that the pickings are good, got it? The other thing about crowds is that it's *safer* to be in gangs. That way, you've got a good chance of having eyes looking everywhere. Some of us keep an eye out for foxes or stoats and weasels, whilst another lot keep an eye on the sky. Well, big though I am, Brendan buzzard will swoop down and have a go at you if you're not careful. It's all right for some birds, like our Ambassador tawny owl for instance. He can turn his head right round backwards, so he can see behind him real quick like.

Lucky him, that's what I caw! So a big gang of noshing birds has got heaps of eyes in all directions. Saves a lot of bother, and stops me from getting indigestion.

Speaking of tummies, well we rooks are very adaptable where the good old grub stakes come in! Me, I'll eat just about anything, alive or dead. 'Oh yuck!' I can hear you say. Hey, now wait a bill minute, you hoomans should be grateful that we eat dead things. I mean, do you *really* want all that smelly stuff all over your fields? Of course not! We just do the garbage collection, that's all.

Oh Gaia, I nearly fluttered off to birdie heaven the other day. I was just drifting quietly over some fields, and I saw the grey snaking line you hoomans zoom along in you funny motor things, far below me. Well, I mean, there it was, a big fat rabbit lying by the side of the ... what do you hoomans call it...? *road*... ah yes. Well, there it was, just lying there. I think one of you hoomans hit it with one of your fast motor things. So I though to myself, *breakfast - mmm*, that's what I thought, so I wafted down on my shining glossy black feathers, and started to nosh on the rabbit. Well, then it happened, another one of your hooman motor things came hurtling towards me, and there I was, sitting in the middle of the road! Oh, Gaia! I cawed for the motor thing to stop, but it didn't. So I only flapped away in the feather of time. That was a close one, I can caw you. You won't catch me doing that again.

Now you might have noticed how shiny my feathers are. I keep them shiny by putting some oil from inside my bill onto each feather. We rooks call that *preening*, but perhaps you hoomans already knew that was what we caw it. The oil keeps the rain out, and also helps us to stop nasty little creepy bugs from getting under our feathers. Every now and then, me and my friends take a bath, and flap our wings all over the place, duck our heads in the water and make a real nice mess. This is great, honestly, a good wash also keeps us clean, and stops little biters and stinging things from taking up house on our bodies.

Come the spring, it's time to get thinking about making baby rooks - family time I call it. I told you about us liking to be in gangs, didn't I? Well, we make our nests in big gangs too. Look at any nice clump of tallish trees with nice spreading branches with open fields nearby, and you'll probably see where we nest. If you look in the winter, when the bronze and yellow leaves have fallen, you can see heaps of our twiggy nests high up in the branches.

They are kind of flat, with lots of dead twigs sticking out all over the place, and sometimes there could be as many as a dozen nests in one tree. Well, some of us nest in evergreen trees like pine trees, and if that's the case, tough luck trying to find where we nest, that's all I can say! Anyway, before the new leaves come on the trees, before the cold frosts and snow have stopped dusting the countryside with white powder, we rooks go back to our old nesting places and start doing some nest repairs.

See, the winter gets kind of windy, if you know what I mean, and we don't have glue to stick the nests together with, so pieces get, well, kind of bashed about, and fall off! Plenty of twigs lying around though, so come February, you'll often see me and my friends carrying twigs to our nests. The lady rooks turn up around then too, and it's time to start dating! Yippee! Arrrgh! What am I cawing? That's when all the really hard work starts. Oh yes, it's fun cawing and showing off, handing the ladies twigs for pressies and that, but once we have chosen a partner, it's all grind and tiredness. Looking after two or three gobbling, yelling youngsters is hard work, I can tell you! They don't give you a moment's peace, and neither do the other parents in the rookery.

Cawing for myself, I don't get it. I mean, when we rooks are in gangs in the fields, just noshing together, we seem to get on pretty well, but once it's nesting time, we seem to go berserk. When I'm not flitting from field to field to get grubs and things for the chicks, I'm sitting near the nest having a row with another rook. Mostly, it's a row about stealing things. You wouldn't believe how lazy some of those blooming young rooks are, the ones making their nests for the first time, I mean. What's wrong with them, that's what I want to know?

I didn't go around stealing other people's twigs from *their* nests, at least, I don't think I did... or did I? Now you hoomans wouldn't rush off to your next door neighbour's house and start pinching their bricks and furniture from right under their beaks, I mean noses, now would you? Oh, it makes me so cross - I guess you've guessed that. Well, come the end of the nesting time, the chicks fly off and we can get some peace.

Last year, my poor feathers got in such a mess. My biggest wing feathers (we call them the *primary* feathers, by the way) got all torn and tattered, and I even lost a few of them. So come the autumn, I had to grow some new ones, most of us do that, you know. It's called a *moult*, and it's a bit like you hoomans deciding to buy some new clothes because your old ones have got holes in them, you know?

I wasn't around at the time, but a long time ago, one of our favourite trees, called the elm, started dying all over the place. You know, the leaves started to go brown in the middle of spring or summer, and they never put on the leaves again. Our Ambassador owl told us birds that this was caused by an insect that laid its eggs in the bark of the elms. These little grubs ate all the nice living sap inside the bark, and killed those great big elms. Now can you imagine what it would be like if your houses started to crumble and fall down? Think about it. Not just a few houses, but a whole village or part of a town or city. Argh! In places where we rooks had used the elms for our nesting places, we were suddenly out of luck! There's no point in nesting in trees that don't put their leaves on for us to hide in, now is there?

You know, I'm not one to boast really, but we rooks are very clever birds, honestly we are. We can cope with lots of changes, and that's what makes us so successful as birds. So, we just found a way to cope with the elm sickness, and found other trees to nest in, but things were really bad for a while there. By the way, I'm not normally this serious, you know. We rooks have a great time just messing about in the air; spinning, diving, sliding and slicing with our jet-black wings. Why, we even have fun with big flocks of jackdaws if they happen to be in the mood to join in.

Well, I really must flit off now. It's time to go back to the rookery and see who's around to caw to. So, dear hooman friends, it's up, up and away for me. See you!

Kimmie the Kestrel

## Kimmie the Kestrel

High! No, not 'H-I', I really mean *high*, 'H-I-G-H!' That's where I was just now, yes, up there, up in the clear blue sky, hovering right above your head. I could see everything. I saw you chatting with Ray rook. Yip! Yip! Even though I was as high up as a tall church spire, I could see every detail of you. I might have tiny eyes, like little black jewels in my head, but I can see better than almost any bird in the world, and that's a fact.

I *love* hovering. You know what hovering is? Are you sure? Hovering is flying but not moving forwards or backwards, not that I can fly backwards anyway! *Kek, kek, kek*! Yip, I can hover by beating my sharp pointed wings really fast, and using my fanned-out tail to help me keep steady and still. Now I'm not the only hawk that can hover, but the chances are that if you see a small brown hawk doing a hover, that's one of us kestrels doing it. There are harriers that can do that as well, and I think you hoomans have even named one of your great big metal flying things after them, haven't you? Yes, you have. It's a flying thing that can hover in one place. How clever of you. I'm a bit offended actually. I mean, you also have those other big flying things with wapping great blades that whizz round and round in the air. What's that? Helicopters? Oh well, if you say so - helicopters - well, why don't you name one of them after me? It's not fair, we kestrels hover just as well as harriers!

Oh, I'd better not get too cross, sorry about that. Yip! We hover a lot, sometimes way up high, and sometimes really quite close to the ground. Why? Guess! No? Well here are some clues for you. First, take a look at my beak. Notice anything interesting about it? Well yes, I know it's small, sillies! Yes, yes, it's pale silvery white with a black very sharp beak, and do I mean sharp! Well, keep that in mind, and take a look at my feet. Hang on, I'll stretch one out for you.

There, can you see now? Look at those pointed claws, neat, eh? Fine yellow legs, nice pale white feathers on my thighs, and yes, you're getting warm. Sharp beak, strong pointed claws. Got it? Well, what do you think we eat? Not fruit, not flowers... yes, we eat animals! Mainly little mice and voles, and sometimes... I'd better whisper this bit... come closer... let me tell you in your ear ...yes, yes... we eat birds as well... sorry... but that's a fact... I had to whisper this because Larry the lapwing is sitting just over there, waiting to talk to you and, to be perfectly honest, I ate one of his chicks last year and I think he suspects something!

Right, so we kestrels eat little mice and voles. Now where do they live? Yip! They live on the ground. Tiny little balls of fluffy brown and grey things, dashing through the grass in the fields. This is why we like to hover, to spy out the land below, to wait for the dash and dither of a mouse far below. Once I see one, I sometimes slip and slide a little lower and hover again, to check on the movement below, just to make sure, to get closer, ready to pounce. Then, when the time is right, I fold my black-tipped wings to my side and fall out of the sky like a stone. So fast, so quiet, so swift, so sure. I seldom miss!

Then I grab the mouse in my sharp claws and kill it. Then I may eat it right there, or sometimes take it away to a safe place in a tree or on a post. So you see, I need that hovering height to spy out the land, and I need my powerful eyes to spot the slightest movement far below. Okay, you've seen my beak and claws... hang on... I'll turn my head towards you, so that you can see my face. Nice, eh? Do you like my nice black whiskers on each side of my cheeks? Kevin, my partner this year, also has black whiskers, but his head is a lovely dove grey, not nut brown like mine.

Now we both have speckled black feathers on brown bodies, but I have many more spots than Kevin. Take a look at my tail, see? I've got lovely bands of black all the way down my tail. Now Kevin doesn't have that. His tail is the same dove grey as his head, with a tip of black. How big am I? Well, I guess I'm about the same size as one of those funny tin cans you hoomans have to spray polish from. There are other hawks that look a bit like me, so I don't blame you if you get me mixed up with them.

But, hey, it's not that hard. For starters, we kestrels are one of the most common of the hawk family and not very shy at that! Oh yes, sparrowhawks, hobbies and merlins look a bit like me, but they aren't so common, and sparrowhawks have very long tails, much longer than mine, and hobbies and merlins are smaller. Why, a merlin is quite tiny really. So don't worry, you'll get the hang of it.

You know, there isn't really anywhere that we kestrels wouldn't be happy hunting and living in. I have friends who even live in the middle of great big hooman cities, like, what do you call it? Oh... London... yes, that's it *Yip*! Kestrels even hunt and nest in London! *Adaptable* that's the hooman word I'm looking for. We can adapt to just about any place. It helps to be adaptable, you know.

When you hoomans built those great big straight flat grey pathways for your motor things to rush along, we were so happy, I can tell you! You were so nice to put all that lovely grass along the banks, and to plant trees and shrubs there too. I often hunt on one of those, I don't know what it's called, but where I hunt, there's a great big sign up and it says 'A38' on it, whatever that means! It's like this see: where there is grass, there are mice. Heaps of them. Yum Yum!

Many sunrises ago, you hoomans did a silly thing. You started to spray smelly stuff on your crops, and the insects ate this stuff and got sick. The mice ate the sick insects, and we ate the mice. The horrid poison stuff was inside the mice, and it made us have lots of problems. Our eggs wouldn't hatch, so we started to lose our numbers. We kestrels didn't have it quite so bad as peregrines and sparrowhawks, but it's a good job you stopped doing that, otherwise we could have died out you see, and that would be a real shame, now wouldn't it?

*Yik, yik, yik, yik!* Just letting Kevin know I'm okay. He's over there, yes, way over there, hovering near those beech trees. He's such a sweetie really. We've been dating since early spring this year, and we raised three lovely chicks together. I met him on one gorgeous late winter morning. He flew right past me, *yickering* and *mewing* with half a field vole in his mouth. Then he settled in a tall tree close by, and bobbed his lovely grey head up and down towards me, calling me to him. Well, I mean, I couldn't resist that, now could I?

So over I swooped, and so you know what? He gave me that delicious vole to eat. Mmmmmmm! Well that was that really. We started to work on the nest right away, mainly little twigs all knitted together, very high up in the tree. We worked very hard on that for a few days, I can *yik* you! Some of us kestrels make our nests in lower places, even holes in old buildings and gaps in church towers in towns and cities. Then, as time passed, and Kevin kept on bringing me more and more nice little things to eat, I found myself laying my first egg, then after a few days two more.

Kevin was very good at giving me plenty of peace and quiet. Any time anything came close to the nest, he would swoop and *yicker* and *kick*! He was quite fierce I can *yik* you. I did most of the sitting on the eggs, though if I needed to find a drink of nice clear water, he would sit on the eggs for me whilst I was away.

My favourite game with Kevin was zooming into the air, and catching food parcels in mid-flight! He'd fly towards me, and then race upwards and toss the piece of food into the space above my head. I'd spin on my wings and make myself almost upside down, reach out a claw, and catch the meat as it fell. Oh, what fun! Well, a lot of sunrises went by, and then the great day came when the first chick cracked the shell of the egg and popped his darling little wet and fluffy head out for the first time. Within two sunrises, the other two hatched as well.

Kevin flew everywhere to catch food for the babies; mice, little you-know-whats, sometimes even a frog or big fat insect. He would drop the food in the nest, and I would tear it into little pieces and feed my babies. After a while though, they got so hungry, that we both had to fly and get them food. By then, the babies could tear up the food themselves, which helped a lot actually. I'm afraid the babies aren't that nice to each other in the nest. I don't know why, but they fight a lot. I have heard that some kestrel babies will starve another one to death, if they are bossy enough. This sounds pretty tough to me, but it happens sometimes. I guess Gaia likes to make sure that the strongest birds get to fly.

Well, we did so well. All three of our chicks got their feathers just fine, and got nice and fat. Then one day, they started to flap their wings, jumping up and down in the nest, especially on days when a nice wind breezed about, and that was that really. The next thing Kevin and me knew, they were all flying! Isn't that marvellous? We kept on feeding them for quite a while, but they soon learned how to catch food of their own.

Well, it's nearly winter now. The big oak trees are covered in leaves very nearly the same colour as my brown feathers. Now I know this might seem a bit soft of me, but Kevin and me still keep close to our babies. Some babies leave home earlier, but this year our babies have stayed with us. Nice really! Mind you, when the really cold weather comes, when there's less to eat, I'm afraid they'll have to flit off, and so will Kevin.

I don't know whether I'll see him again next year, maybe, maybe not. Ooooo, can you hear that? Mmm, my little tummy is growling. I must go and fly round my beat soon to find something to eat. My beat? Oh, that's what I call the area where I fly. Kevin and me keep our beady black eyes out for those oh-so naughty birds that think they own everywhere. Well, they jolly well don't own the bit we hunt on, so they'd better not try to move in on us!

This has been a lot of fun, *yicking* to you, I mean. I do hope you'll keep an eye on Kevin and me, and when he's gone, try to spot me zooming low over a field, or hovering by one of your big long grey tracks for your motor things. I'll keep an eye on you too! And if I'm sure that you mean me no harm, I'll settle into a hoover and give you a long flickering wave of my wings, okay?

Larry the Lapwing

## Larry the Lapwing

Peewit! Peewit! Peewit!

Hey there hoomans! How ya doin? Strewth, I dunno how you can stand listening to all that yickering from Kimmie kestrel. I'll bet you've got a yucky feeling in your tummies right now, eh? I mean what has *she* got to *yik* about except clawing things, tearing things, pouncing on things, blood, guts, and stuff like that, eh? It's enough to make you go as green as me and moult your feathers in sheer fright! Eeeow! Eeeeeee, wit!

Duh, how silly of me, you haven't got feathers have you? Well, not sticking out of your skin anyway. In your what? In your *pillows* and *duvets*? What on grass is that? What, you *go to sleep with them*? You've got to be kidding? You actually stuff feathers in your pillows and put your heads on them? Well, I always wondered about you hoomans, you do such funny things. Well, I'm not going to make you sick, so there. I won't be telling you gory and yucky stories about blood and guts.

See, so far as nosh goes, I like bugs. Whoops, I guess that's a bit yucky too, isn't it? When I say bugs, I mean that we feed on insects mainly, anything that creeps in the grass and maybe the odd worm if any of them are silly enough to pop their heads out of the ground. That's why you can see so many of us in the fields, just walking on our long legs, and tipping our bodies forward to sticky-beak into the ground and grass. I don't even bend my neck, just tip forward, all stiff like and snap up the grubs. Yum yum!

Now I hope you don't think that I've got a big head or anything like that, but lapwings have something that most other birds don't have. I wonder if you have noticed? Well? Look at my head. Notice anything? Hang on, I'll help you... I'll just make a frown with my muscles in the top of my head and hey presto! Mmm, see? I have a *crest*! Yes, a few feathers that stick out from the top of my head, like little aerials!

Hey, I dunno why we have them! All I know is that they're great for making signs with. Ya know, stick 'em up in the air and bob your head and birds notice that! I mean, you hoomans stick your arms up in the air when you wave to people don't you? Well, stands to reason then, if we have a little tuft of feathers on top of our heads, we're gonna wave with them. My crest is a bit longer than the lady lapwing plumes, but you probably wouldn't be able to see that in the fields.

And another thing, I know we guys look the same as the gals, but my face is a lot blacker than a lady lapwing's face. They have more white on them, see? Otherwise, we look very much alike, which makes it tough on you hoomans to know which is which, I guess. Now I know you hoomans like learning big words, neat, I think! Well, we lapwings are very comfy in big crowds. You'll often see great whopping gangs of us in the fields, especially in the colder months.

Now here's the thing, you hoomans have a nice word for that, you know, for things that are friendly and that like to get in big bunches. Want to know what it is? *Gregarious.* Now there's a nice word, that's what we are, gregarious. We don't fight when we are in a crowd, well, not much any-way. We just hop around and nosh, and the rest of the time, we just, well, stand around, all stiff and straight like. Hey, I guess this is funny, but we do a lot of standing about then we get a sudden urge, like we've been bitten by an ant, and suddenly run like crazy!

Look, I dunno, it just happens, okay. You'd think we were nervous if I didn't tell you that we just like to dash sometimes. Well, actually we *are* a bit nervous as a matter of fact. I mean, I don't mind lapwings, but I do get a bit on the edgy side when you lot come clomping and stomping in the fields and meadows. To be honest, you lot scare me a bit, so don't expect me to doddle up and sit at your feet and ask for a tickle!

When we fly, you might have noticed that we have very big wings, kind of flat on the outer edges. Well thank Gaia - we need those big wings, 'cos we just love flying. In the times when Jack Frost or Sarah Snow come along, things get tough for us. Have you ever thought what it's like to get your beak into soil that's as hard as rock? You won't see *me* bending and breaking my beak by pranging it into soil stiff with frost and ice, I can *wit* you! This is the time when we take a flight together in very big bunches.

Wit, peewit. We just take to the air, and flap off to find somewhere a little warmer, sometimes further south. A big movement of birds like that is called *migration*, but maybe you already know that word? Oh wow, those winters! They are very tough on us birds. At night time, we stay in big bunches and just squat in the fields and sleep for a while. Sometimes, when the moon gets very big and bright, a few of us will have a midnight feast, but that doesn't happen very often, to be honest.

I love it when the spring comes along, *eee-wit*! Great, I reckon! That's when I can really show off my skills as a flyer. You ever been to one of those funfair things? Ever been on what you hoomans call a roller coaster? You know, when you go up real high, and then zoom down to earth and your tummy stays behind and catches you up later? Fun, eh? Well, I do that in the spring! No, sillies, I don't go to funfairs, but I do fly up in the air, and then fold my wings to my side and dive straight down. Sometimes I pull out of the dive right at the last minute, just before I would hit the ground.

Lady lapwings just love my aerial stunts. It's my best feature, you know. Best flyers attract the best ladies. And I fairly *wit* my wits with screaming and *peewitting*! That's why you call us peewits, I guess. My other name, lapwing? Hmmm, let me see, now I wonder how you got that name? Oh *peeeeewit*! I've got it, I've really got it. Of course, that's it! I can make a noise with my wing-tip feathers, like a whip of rope whistling through the air, in fast quick beats... *whupp-whupp-whup-whup*... maybe that's why you call us lapwings? Mind you, I reckon you should have called us *whupwings*, but I guess that's none of my business, right?

We've got another name too, green plover. *Green plover*? Well, I *peewit* you! Okay we are green in colour, but did you really *have* to mix us up with all those other plovers, like golden plover, ringed plover, and all that? Oh, I see, I forgot. You hoomans have family names too. Like that guy Edward, who's been translating Birdish into English for you. I mean, he's called *Cowie* right? And there are lots of Cowies, right. Oh, I get it! Plover is our family name. Duh, how silly of me. Well, okay, I guess it's okay to call me green plover then, 'cos plover is like my family name. I'll let you off this time!

Now where was I... oh yeah... the spring! *Peeeeee*! Yes, that's when I do some real fancy flying. You know, we have a lot of wisdom, us birds, lots of stories. My dad told me that once, long ago, we lapwings had a rough time here. You hoomans got some really nasty stuff and sprayed it on your crops right? What do you mean, 'oh, not again'? Someone else been *witting* to you about pesticides? Oh yes, of course, Kimmie the kestrel. Well, they had the same problem.

See, it's like this. Lapwings eat the very insects that you

hoomans were killing with your poisons. Ugh, what yucky stuff! This stuff got into our bodies and made us go like crazy, yeah, crazy. We began to crash in our show-off flights. Some of us didn't know how to pull out of a dive any more - just went straight into the ground and broke our necks. Then there was the problem with eggs that wouldn't hatch - whoops - this is getting really yucky, and I promised I wouldn't make you get sick! It's okay now, you stopped using that horrid stuff and we seem to be safe now.

Right, back to that big spring field. Well, get the picture. There was I zooming about in the sky, turning and spinning, *witting* and wing-*whupping* all over the place. And down below, far below, like little specks of green jade, the ladies were looking up at me. Oh no! I thinks to myself, time for a quick dive and a flash of my bright eyes at those ladies, so I did just that. Over and over again. Of course, other blokes like me were doin' it as well, but hey! I'm super-wing!

Well, there was this one lady, Loretta lapwing. Oh, hoomans, what a chick! Fell in love like a ... well, fell for her in a big way... get it? *Wit-wit-wit-pu-wee-wit*! What a joke... *fell* for her... got it... Wow... I'm smart! She gave me one of those looks, ah, yes, made my crest stand on edge I can tell you. Next thing I knew, I was snuggling up to her and we were on our first date.

Oh hoomans, I knew what to do next. I dashed off to look for a nice little hollow in the ground. I found a great one. Some cows had been stomping in the meadow, and left hoof-marks in the most convenient spots. So I squatted down, fluffed out my feathers, and started to spin round and round, kicking with my feet all the time. You'd have lauged. There I was, going round and round, kicking the soil out on every side, making like a... well... making like a fruit bowl in the ground. Next thing I remember is that I started to collect pieces of grass, and lined the scrape I made.

Then Loretta came right over, and hey presto! One, two, three, four eggs! Oh Gaia! What lovely eggs, what a lovely shape; pointed at one end, fat on the other, creamy white, but covered in blobs and streaks of green, brown, dark red and black. So then, Loretta wits to me, 'Right Larry!' she says, 'buzz off!' *Buzz off*? Hey, I mean, I thought she meant like really buzz off, but actually she just meant for me to stand on guard, keep an eye out for interfering busybodies, or those nasty foxes and stoats. Anything that likes to nosh on eggs, got it?

Then, oh Gaia! One by one, our little darlin's hatched. What clever little things they were too. Right away, they started flitting about, and feeding for themselves. How very considerate of them, saved me so much time and energy! Ya see, lapwing babies are born covered in fluff, and they can see just fine, right from birth. I feel so sorry for those poor birds that have ugly little bundles of fluffy noshers to feed.

Mind you, it ain't easy looking after a small gang of youngsters that flit and zoom all over the place. Loretta and me had a real scare one day. Over the far side of the field, we saw this red fox coming right towards us. Oh, shiver my plumes! Up I gets, hopping and flapping, pretending like I had a broken wing. *Oh ho*! thinks the fox, nosh time! I had him fooled. He just kept on following me! Meanwhile, the chicks crouched low down, flat and still, and Loretta flipped and flapped over the fox's sneaky head. Next thing *he* knew, I was up in the air, just witting at him. Worked a treat.

Smart Larry, that's me. And hey, want to hear something even smarter? Well, cop this one then. Once, I saw a weasel sliding and slithering close to my little darlings, so what do I do? I start hopping and flipping and sneak over some way from the chicks, and take off and settle, like that's where my nest is. Then I get real close to the ground and make little *peeping* sounds, just like my babies. Got it?

Yeah, the weasel thinks I have the chicks with me, so over she comes, sliding and slithering some more. Then I flew up suddenly, just before she got to me, and oh Gaia, I have her heaps. Was she cross? Was she just! Peeeeewit, peeeewit! Time to go, I'm afraid, got to let Pamela have her time with you and anyway, I'm hungry again, and just longing to loop the loop. Have a nice day! Bye!

Pamela the Partridge

## Pamela the Partridge

...I know! Ooo yes, well she had such a cheek... I told her that... yes... I know... well she shouldn't have *keeer-rricked* at all really... I know... hmmm... yes, well she would interfere... you can't stop her, you know... mmm... I know... she's such a busy-fluffer... sticking her beak in where it's not wanted... no... really? She *keeerrricked* that, did she... somebirdy should tell her to shut up, once in a while... I know... hang on a flap or two...yes... can I help you? What's that... you want to talk to me? Oh dear, I'm busy *skerrrring* to my dear friend right now. Oh... you can't wait all day? Oh dear... just a minute. Mmmm... I know... she never used to be like that... it's his fault you know... he's so bossy... I know... look I'm sorry, but I *have* to stop now... there's a hooman over there waiting to talk to me... *I know*... scary stuff hoomans... I know... but they won't go away... they say that I *have* to talk to them... oh my!... Oh my dear... I remember now... I am supposed to talk to this hooman for a while... Ambassador owl's orders, I know... but what can a poor partridge do? Well, I mean to *kteeerrrr*!

Okay, I'm ready now. Sorry about that, I quite forgot I had to talk with you. Now, how can I help you? Oh, you'd like to stay for a little while? At my place, oo, let's see if we have any vacancies, oh... you don't want to stay overnight? Oh, I know, you just want a chat... well... I know. Okay, what do you want to know? Ooooo, *kch-kch-kch*! silly me... you want to know about partridges... of course you do!

Well, really, what can I *kcheerrrrr*? It's a bit sad, yes, I know, well we partridges aren't very common you see. Well, I'm not *common* at all, not like *some* birds I could mention. No, I was just joking, I mean that we have

185

become very scarce you know. Well, it's all your fault really. You have taken away so many fields, with tall grasses, and lots of trees, hedges and bushes close by. That's what we like, see. There used to be millions of us about, but we haven't got enough quiet places anymore, so I'm afraid you're lucky to see me at all! Well, we partridges don't fly much, but live most of the time on the ground, like our cousins the pheasants.

When I do fly, it's only a little bit off the ground. I don't like heights - gives me vertigo, you know! Hmmmmmm, just a straight little flight on fast-beating wings, straight as a ruler and then I dip down again and dive for cover. Shy you see! Most of the time, we stay in close little parties. I think you hoomans call that *coveys*, that's family groups to you. When we aren't in our little family parties, we get in bigger flocks and rush about secretly and quietly in the undergrowth.

I run about a lot, well, we all do. I don't like rough ground mind, I keep on tripping over if the ground is rough. That's why we like nice flat fields, especially nice ploughed and harrowed ones.

Now, I reckon I look pretty really, well both mummy and daddy partridges do. I don't have so much orange on my face as the gentlemen partridges do, and my breast is much darker. But we all have such lovely mottled feathers, lovely colours if you ever get close to one of us. Mind you, that would be hard; we don't like hoomans much.

Oh, come on now, *you* wouldn't like animals that dug up your gardens and parks, and who sent little bits of metal in the air that knocked you dead, now would you? You know what I mean, *guns*. Oh, I know, horrible really. It's terrible isn't it? I know, the best view of our feathers is in one of your butcher's shops. Oooo, I *kcheerrrrrr*! I think you hoomans used to think that we partridges ate all your corn and seeds, *we don't*! Mostly, I like to eat little insects that I find in the grass by pecking and probing with my beak, which I hope you've noticed is the same nice grey as the feathers on my shoulders.

Nesting time? Oh dear, that's a bit confusing really. Well it is at first, there's often so many gentlemen partridges about, all trying to dance with you at the same time. It gets a real problem knowing which of them you like the most, you know. Oh, well, we get things sorted out eventually and look for a nice hollow in the bushes, deep inside big tufts of grass, or inside a big piece of hedge.

Then we sometimes scrabble and scratch to make the hollow ground a little deeper, and line the bottom of it with grass and leaves. Mmm, I know, of course we hide the nest, I mean, seeing that we don't fly much, there are heaps of things that would gobble me or my chicks up. Oh don't *ktcheeerrrr* to me about gentlemen partridges! Cute they may be, but when it comes to nest-building and sitting on the eggs, well, what can I say? *Lazy*, that's the word. They don't do a thing. And there am I sitting on heaps of eggs, yes, heaps of them, yes, all on my own. Oh well, Percy did help a bit when the chicks hatched, and he was helpful once we started to move the chicks on to start feeding.

Oh, my dears, you would *ktcheeeerrrrtter* if you could see us then! There was I, pattering along in front of a little line of darlings, with Percy taking up the rear, you know, making sure that the ones at the back kept in line, making sure that nothing sneaked up behind us, sweet that, I suppose, I know! Mmmm, I know what you'd think if you heard me and Percy chatting with our chicks, yes I do, really. You'd hear me going chook! *Chook! Chook! Chook!* And you'd be clever in thinking that a partridge can sound like one of your hooman chickens.

Well, have I got news for you! Wait for it, hmmm, yes, chickens and partridges are related. Though why on earth our chooky cousins should be so stupid as to let you lot pen them up and lay eggs for *you* to eat, I can't imagine. I mean, what a silly thing to do. I don't think they have a brain in their heads, silly things, that's what I was *kcheer-rrrrng* about to Patty Partridge just now, I know, she agrees with me, daft we all call it. Mind you, Patty is right, if you do keep chickens, you'll get some good ideas about how we partridges live, so I guess we should be thankful for that, now shouldn't we?

Well, nice though this is, I really must get back to my chattering - whoops - I mean work! Got so much to chatter about - whoops - I mean so much work to do. See you later... she didn't? really? Oh I *ktcheerrrr*... when was that? What today? Well... what did you do? Oh I know...I would have as well... it's enough to make you want to fly... I know... well, I told her that she should go for a walk and settle down... and mind her own business... she didn't? I know... well that's what I think too... she should know better... scuttering about like... somebirdy's got to tell her... well I could if you like... I know... I...

Simon the Skylark

# Simon the Skylark

Notthatanybodyisaskingme... nottahtanybodyisaskingme... notthatany-
bodyisaskingmetoexplainhowthesonggoes... notthatanybodyisasking-
mehowthesonggoeswhenupheresohighinthesky...

Hello there. I'm sorry, I forgot to slow down, to make each word clear for you. It's a habit... it's a habit that... it's a habit that... It's a habit that I have... it's a habit that I have when... it's a habit that I have when I sing my songs, I just keep adding sounds all the time and I don't even think about stopping and putting full stops and commas in.

But I'm a nice bird, really, so I'll make things easier, and slow down for you. I hear that you have been chirruping to lots of birds? Well, that *is* nice! I expect that I'm one of the smallest birds you have met, eh? I'm not much bigger than a sparrow really, and yes, you could hold me in your hands and there'd be plenty of room for me to snuggle into. Now I come to think of it, I do look a bit like a sparrow, but to be honest, you'd never catch a sparrow doing what Simon the skylark does!

Yes, I'm kind of brown all over, with lots of speckled feathers, but I'm sort of pale in colour really, especially round my face. Hmmm... well, yes, I *do* have something in common with Larry lapwing. Can you guess? It's right on the top of my head... yes, I have a crest too. Not little feathers though that stick up like they haven't been combed. My crest is thicker and I only lift it up when I am singing or showing off or getting tough with other larks!

Oh, I belong in the fields all right! Yes, the more open the better. And just like Larry, I don't like little fields with hedges close by either. I like a nice open view and lots of shortish grass as well. In fact, I guess it's fair to say that we larks like the same kind of place that lapwings do. You know the name we have for the place where you can find us living? You don't? Oh well. It's *habitat*. Do try to remember that big word, it helps 'cos that's the name given to the special places where an animal can be found. My habitat is open fields and moors, and some of us like the grasses that grow on sand dunes by the seaside.

Take me, for example. I live close to the sea at Dawlish in Devon. Ever heard of it? Well, there's lots of nice short grass growing on the soft sand. You hoomans have made some funny things there too. You dig little holes in the grass and stick strange sticks in the holes with little flags on top. Then you hoomans come along with long thin bags with lots of sticks in them, and put little white eggs on the ground and hit them all over the place. What is that? What is that all about? Oh, well, perhaps I shouldn't ask really, I was just curious.

Anyway, you keep that grass nice and short and we larks like short grass, so there. Why? Well, you know, grass is a great place to find little bugs and other insect things to eat. Not that I eat things from the grass only. I don't mind leaping and flitting in the air to snap up the odd flying little thing. It's just nice to eat in private that's all, so I really do prefer to get my food on the ground. I expect everybirdie has been showing off a bit to you, eh? I'll bet they keep on saying that they are the prettiest, smartest, biggest, fiercest, fastest bird and all that?

Well, I can't think of anything to boast about. I suppose the most wonderful thing that I do is to fly into the sky and sing and sing and sing! I do this in the spring mostly. Well, that's a really special time for birds you know. When the spring comes it gets warmer, and the sky is sometimes blue and clear. That's when the grasses grow a little taller, and the insects start to get about all over the place. In the spring, that's when the most food is about, right into the summer.

So come the spring, and larks start larking about! It's different then; our crests grow a little longer, and we start to look at, well, to oggle at lady larks, and that's a fact. There's no way I can tell you how to recognise a lady lark, we look so much alike really. Anyway, during the winter months, we just hang around in our special habitat. Yep, just hang about, ladies and guys all mixed up. We don't gather in big flocks like lapwings, but here at Dawlish, if you have acute and sharp eyes, you could expect to see several of us all in the same place, just hopping about in the short grass or flying about a little, from insect cafe to insect cafe!

In spring, things get hot in more ways than one. When it comes to starting families, well, there's no point in denying it, we aren't so happy to have other guys on our patch. Each of us needs to find a mate, to make lots of baby larks and, I don't know about you, but I'm not keen on sharing my partner with another lark, so there! So what I do, is to look for a favourite patch of grass, and start to get my voice ready to defend it. Yep, I meant that, *defend* it. This special patch of mine, is going to be *mine* for the family season. We call this *territory*, now did you know that?

If there were too many larks in my territory, they'd eat all the food, and that's no good when you've got a hungry family of little beaks to stuff! Now because we like flat ground and ground that is hard to see us in, there's not much point in advertising where I am on the ground is there? So what I do is, flap my wings quite quickly and start to float up into the sky, hovering and ascending, up, hover, up a bit more, hover again, until I am high up in the sky, almost as high as the clouds.

I sing all the time. I sing lovely music, lush phrases. I don't stop... I just keep on babbling and fluting all the time. I can see right down below me, and hover over my patch.

The ladies look up, and listen, so it's jolly important to make sure that I fly well and sing even better than I fly. When I get to the top of my flying patch in the air, I suddenly stop singing, fold my wings and float down in a lovely curved dip towards the soft green grass below. Oh, what a feeling!

Sometimes, I sing little bits of music like a flute going from high to low. I like doing that, just as I reach close to the ground. Now this year, I was doing just that, on a fine spring morning, and far below me, I saw a gorgeous lady lark, looking up at me. I swelled my feathers and sang my little feet off! When I reached the ground, there she was, right in the middle of my territory, looking at me, all lush and friendly like. Sylvia is a lovely lark, and oh Gaia, did she like the way I larked!

Next thing, was to find a hollow in the ground, a nice one with an arch of stems over it, a nice shelter of green to hide the nest in. Then we started to weave and wind some fine grass stems together to make our little nest. Now, it's nice of you hoomans to be inquisitive, but hey, I'm not that stupid you know. I'm not going to show you where my nest is. I have a special trick to fix things so that nothing can find where Sylvia and me nest.

It's easy really. I fly down from the sky, and settle on the ground some way away from the nest. Neat, eh? Yep, you see, that way, a naughty animal that might like to eat my babies will think that I have settled right on top of the nest. Well, tough luck! What I do is to flap down and then run along in the shady grass, and sneak into the nest, yards and yards from where I flew down to. And 'cos I'm very cautious, I do the same when I leave the nest. Yep, I run along the ground and *then* take off up into the air.

We had five babies last spring. If anything did get too close, we'd both get into the air, or flap along the ground and make like we were wounded, you know, pretending like we had a broken wing... oh you *knew* that... yes, of course, Larry does that trick! Well, the babies grew very fast and we fed them heaps of little flies. Then they had a real job, when they started to get their proper feathers. It's hard to learn to fly when you have to start from the ground, but they've managed just fine.

Now I do think that it's interesting that some birds are more common than other ones. I mean, there are far fewer larks than there are sparrows. I asked our Ambassador owl about that and he told me that the number of birds 'are limited by habitat types'. I wish he wouldn't come out with those fancy sentences. I just didn't follow what he was getting at, you see!

Anyway, he was kind enough to explain that all birds have different eating habits and that our bodies are different shapes and colours to make sure that we all know who goes where and why. I started to get his point then. I mean, we larks don't eat fish, so there's not much point in us having swimming feet, or living on a river bank, now is there? No, each bird has a different lifestyle so we each have special habitats to live in.

It's because we larks like insects and open spaces that makes us a little hard to find on one of your hooman walks. In fact, you hoomans are a bit greedy you know. A long time ago, there used to be even more fields and moors with shortish grass on them, but you built your houses on them, or changed them into little fields and that meant that larks had to make do with less space to live in.

I know I shouldn't complain, I was just trying to tell you why larks aren't common. Mind you, wherever there *is* a lot of big wide open space, with lush green grasses, you'll probably find larks. That Edward Cowie guy told me that he saw lots of larks on somewhere called Salisbury Plain.

Now I don't know where that is, but from what I can gather, there's heaps of open space there, which is why the sky is full of singing larks.

You know, I don't speak hooman, but I hear that you have nice names for collections of birds. How nice of you! I mean, a *charm* of finches is about right. Hmmm, a *raft* of ducks sounds nice too. But when I heard about what you call collections of larks, I was just thrilled - well, *trilled* actually! An *exaltation* of larks! How cute! I understand that exalt means to lift up, to raise your spirits and feel, well, kind of high. Wow, that's really a nice one. Well, it's time for me to exalt off, or should I say exalt *up*?

See you... seeyoulater... seeyoulaterthen... seeyoulaterthensometime.

Maggie the Magpie

## Maggie the Magpie

Whatcha! Whatchit! Watchout! How ya doin? okay?

Saved the best to last, eh? Smart hoomans, got good taste, eh? Yeah, can't better a magpie, that's for sure. Real class here... real... oh what's the common word? Help me, yeah, come on, what's the best word for magpie? Brilliant... beautiful... bold... brassy... bashful... bumptious... bright... bossy...

Hey! Watchit! You were doin' just fine until you got to the 'bossy' bit. Me? MOI?

BOSSY?

WHO TOLD YOU THAT?

COME ON NOW, WHO WAS IT?

BOSSY?

NEVER!

NOT ME!

Oh, that's the trouble with you hoomans. You see everything in black and white! Ch-ch-ch-ch! Well of course you do, that's what magpies *are* - black and white, I mean!

Let me tell you a tale, ch-ch-ch-ch! I mean, let me *show* you a tail! Take a look at this, my tail's longer than my body. Useful for steering my body in flight, ya know! And by the way, I know I said that I was black and white, well, that's a bit of a fib actually. If you see me in bright sunlight or close up - you'll see that I have a lot of blue in my feathers, and purple and red as well as greens. See, it's like this, my feathers have a lot of oil in them, and this oil makes the light bring out all the colours of the rainbow, especially blue.

I know a thing or two, you know, I know what this is called, I bet you won't remember this - *iridescence*. How about that?  And hey, I'll bet you *didn't* know that magpies don't all have the same amount of black and white?  The strongest and most dominant of us have much bolder markings - I said BOLDER, not balder!  You can leave the baldness bit to coots and rooks!  Otherwise, I guess the guys and gals look very much alike to you lot!

Oh Gaia, you hoomans do yucky things, you even used to cook us in your pies, *ouch*!  Well, nowadays, I guess we magpies have a slightly better reputation, though I'd like to have a peck or two at that composer hooman, what's his name?  A hooman from Italy, I think ya know, he wrote some moosik for some singers to sing, a love story I think - yuck - you sloppy lot!  Well, this hooman wrote this piece see, what's it called?  Ah yes, *The Thievish Magpie*!

## WELL I ASK YOU!

Where *did* you get the idea that we pinched things?  Oh right, well, yeah, we *do* like pretty bright things like flower petals and bright seeds and jewellery - whoops!  That slipped out, better not leave any flashy rings lying around. Come nesting time and I'd be on to that in a flash of my black and white body!

Anyway, that composer hooman, what's his name... Ross Heany...  that's it...  Rossini...  that's the guy...  he'd have been in trouble with *me*, I can tell you.  What a feather.  Oh well, if you hoomans like it that's your business. And another thing I've been beaking to ask you is about that stuff, 'one for sorrow, two for joy', and all that stuff - hey, what the Gaia does *that* mean?  I don't get it, you mean that you really think we magpies bring you sorrow or joy?  COME OFF IT!

Mind you, there's no smoke without that hot yellow stuff, I mean, we *do* usually hang around in ones, twos, threes and fours, seldom in a bigger gang than that, who needs to?  There ain't a bird that's tougher than us lot and there ain't a bird with more guts than me, I ain't scared of you either, so there. Well, smarty fluffs... whoops, I mean smarty-pants... what family do we magpies belong to, eh? That got you thinking, I'll bet. Let me help you, poor things, imagine me without a tail. Look at my beak, strong and big, and my feet, strong and black, and my eyes, bold and bright, and my size. Remind you of anything? Yeeehoooooooooo! Ch-ch-ch-ch-shzeeeeew! You got me! Yeah, I belong to the crow family. Right on!

But the crows ain't so smart as me, so don't believe them if they caw to you that they are! I'm intelligent, that's what I am. Take nesting time for instance. Me and Maurice found a nice big prickly sharp blackthorn bush this year, to build in. Smart, eh? Why? Well, what do black-thorns have a lot of? Prickles, spines, tearing and spiking thorns, that's what! Try getting your sneaky hands into those then! Yeeeeeouch!

Yeah, nice sharp pointed spines to keep busybodies out, see? Then Maurice and me flew down in our nice curving flight, and found some nice big pieces of sticky yucky mud, and went back into the bush, and wedged it into a corner of a branch. Then we got some nice big sticks and shoved them into the mud, flat like, to make a platform. Then the weaving *really* started! Bit by bit, we built a great big cup and just kept on going to make a curved roof over the top, about three times as big as one of your hooman footballs, with just a neat little hole to squeeze into.

The rest's easy, laid four eggs, we both helped to keep them warm and fed them when the flipping greedy little chicks hatched out! What? Oh, I forgot, yeah, food! Well, my little hooman darlin's, *anything* that moves and even yucky things that are dead. All the same to us magpies, though our little darlin's prefer freshly killed meat and insects, to be honest. I realise that this all sounds like magpies are toughies. Well, I guess that's right, but we don't get tough just for fun you know.

Everything that we birds do is to a plan. If we eat things that are lying about rotting, or going for free, we are cleaning things up see and *when* we kill things, we do it quickly. It's just to keep going, to keep our families alive and well. Back to the nest... hmmm... well, yes, it *is* a bit tight in there! I mean, my tail does have to wind round me a bit to sit on the eggs, but hey, no problem. That's what it's meant to do.

Everything is just made to make us all more clever at living. We call that *survival*, right? So we all get clever in different ways, but SOME OF US ARE CLEVERER THAN OTHERS... MAYBE!

Magpies have found a way to fit in just about anywhere, even in the middle of your hooman towns and cities. In fact, there's heaps of good nosh in cities. Just give us a few spiky trees and we are happy! Well my little chooks, my time's my own, and I've got a lot of pilfering, raiding, arguing, nicking, pinching, scrapping, playing, screeching, bullying to do, so if you don't mind, I'm going to hop it right now.

Our Ambassador gets to have the last word, I hope he's pleased with what we've all done, getting to know you lot better, and you lot us, and here's my final thought for you hoomans. Remember this, the next time you start watching birds, watch out 'cos there's an awful lot of us birds that spend a lot of time
WATCHING YOU!
GOT IT?
WELL?

## By the Way!

A last hoot from me!

Yoooooo-hoooooo! I did promise yoo-hoo lovely hoomans that I'd have the last hoot in this boo-hook. Now that yoo-hoo have read this boo-hook, yoo-hoo can honestly say that yoo-hoo are getting too-hoo be quite an expert on British birds. Well done!

But yoo-hoo know, I mentioned that there are some great organisations (wow, what a *big* hooman word!) that doo-hoo a lot too-hoo help us birds too-hoo survive and flourish. Some of them will be listed in your hooman phone boo-hooks and some won't be. I hooted too-hoo Edward the hooman about this, and we think that it woo-hood be a great idea if yoo-hoo got in touch with the *biggest* organisation in this country, because they will be just delighted too-hoo have yoo-hoo join their club, no matter how old yoo-hoo are! So I am going too-hoo put their address at the end of this final letter, okay?

By the way, great news! Edward the hooman and me are getting too-hoogether too-hoo write another boo-hook on British birds, called '*More Birds' Talk*'. We found heaps more birds whoo-hoo are just bursting too-hoo tell their stories too-hoo yoo-hoo too-hoo. And here's greater news. Guess what? The Birdograph works just fine with furry animals and even insects as well, so we might even get some of them along in some boo-hooks later.

Great too-hoo have hooted with yoo-hoo all, and see yoo-hoo later, right?

All the best,

Bill!

William Isaac Stephen Eric Owl
Ambassador to Birds of Britain
The Larch Tree Residence
Devon
England


PS  Here's that address!
The Royal Society for the Protection of Birds
RSPB Headquarters
The Lodge
Sandy
Bedfordshire SG19 2DL

Telephone:  01767 680551
Web site: http://www.rspb.org.uk